Jacob T. Marley

R. WILLIAM BENNETT

SHADOW
MOUNTAIN

In various places throughout the manuscript, actual quotations from
A Christmas Carol, by Charles Dickens, have been included. These
passages appear exactly as they did in the original, with no alterations
to modernize spelling or punctuation.

First printing in hardbound 2011
First printing in paperbound 2014

Visit us at ShadowMountain.com

Library of Congress Cataloging-in-Publication Data
Bennett, R. William, author.
   Jacob T. Marley / R. William Bennett.
        pages cm
   Summary: "A parallel account to Charles Dickens's classic *A Christmas
Carol*, recounting events from the point of view of Scrooge's old partner,
Jacob Marley"—Provided by publisher.
   ISBN 978-1-59038-351-3 (hardbound : alk. paper)
   ISBN 978-1-60907-915-4 (paperbound)
   1. Marley, Jacob (Fictitious character)—Fiction. I. Dickens, Charles,
1812–1870. Christmas carol. Based on: II. Title.
   PS3602.E66449J33 2011
   813'.6—dc22   2011022427

Printed in the United States of America
Publishers Printing, Salt Lake City, UT

10 9 8 7 6 5 4 3 2 1

To C.D.,
our faithful Friend
and Servant,
who taught us all
how to keep Christmas.

PREFACE

Ebenezer Scrooge's visit with the four ghosts and his subsequent redemption is well-known throughout the world. Indeed, it has become quite a celebrated tradition to relive the tale every year at Christmastime, disliking the old man at first, filling with compassion as we see him suffer the realization of his opportunities lost, and springing forth with Ebenezer in unrestrained joy in his bedchamber on that Christmas morning as he realizes he has yet another chance to use his earthly time to do good.

Yet with more sobriety we recall an essential player in this drama, paid homage by Scrooge after he proclaims his commitment to alter his path. "O Jacob Marley!

Heaven and the Christmas-time be praised for this! I say it on my knees, old Jacob, on my knees!"

What of old Jacob? We know he was a "good man of business," from Scrooge's corrupted view of life. There is a small mention of his dress and hair. We also know, by Marley's own account, given as he began the process of turning Scrooge, that he regretted the life he lived. Most important, although he came from a world in which spirits of men were consigned to wander the earth, feeling the pain of remorse but having no access to the balm of reparative action, he was able to procure for Scrooge the visits of the three spirits as a final warning to avoid his own fate. In fact, Marley was able to provide the introduction to that most impactful night personally to Ebenezer in a brief but life-changing encounter. From that moment, Jacob is but a memory, properly acclaimed by Scrooge in the first morning of his new life.

Who was this man? Why was he so evil? Why did he in fact get to visit Scrooge and usher in the experience that changed first Ebenezer and then so many of our lives? Why did Scrooge get a final chance to change and not Jacob Marley?

Or did he?

I

Marley's death was but a beginning. To those of us still mingling with the living, death may seem quite a terminal affair, yet in its vacuum new possibilities spring forth, not just for those left behind but for the dead as well. Marley's death did, in fact, represent a beginning for several people. As the grand old narrator has so deftly and pleasantly informed us, it was at first a long, slow beginning of the transformation of one Ebenezer Scrooge. Indeed, he needed to percolate for seven long years, steeping himself in the boiling liquid of greed and avarice, before he was ready for that dreadful, wonderful night that began with Marley's ghostly visit. It was a beginning for many kind souls who surrounded Scrooge's life: Bob Cratchit, Nephew Fred, Tiny Tim, and even the boy who tried to sing a carol for Ebenezer outside the countinghouse on that Christmas Eve. For in each of those good folk, small seeds of ideas, known by some as inspiration, by others as compassion or goodly character, moved them to play a role in the redemption of the old, miserly Scrooge. And finally, it was a beginning for the detestable Jacob Marley himself.

Now, I suppose that one might be convinced, after some debate on semantics, of the nature of this event being a beginning for each of those aforementioned. Each, that is, but Jacob Marley. True, we know from the account of Scrooge that Jacob was doomed to wander the earth, visiting those he had not helped and feeling the anguish of what might have been, had he been the man he might. But that feels a bit more like an eternal ending rather than anything that deserves to be placed at the start of a conversation.

However, it was a most remarkable beginning for Jacob. For there was a great deal more happening to him than Scrooge could see from his chair by the fire in his bedroom. In fact, the greatest effect Jacob Thelonius

Marley would have on this world would begin on Christmas Eve in the moments before he would leave his corpse behind and would stretch until . . .

Well, this is our story . . .

To understand the time between Jacob's death and his wispy visit with Ebenezer in the bedroom with the old Dutch tiles showing the scenes of Bible stories, one must go back and see what path led him to this spot wherein he was permitted to frighten Scrooge for his own good. It is said in heaven that a record is kept of men's lives. If that be so, if it truly is important enough for heaven to document the moments of our existence, certainly it must be important enough for us to at least reference selected segments from that story to gain insight on how the man came to be who he was. For the corrupt character of Jacob Thelonius Marley was not made by deity; rather, it was a morbid distortion of who he had started out to be, a sad and rough-hewn statue chipped to existence from the stone of his potential by choice after choice of the man himself.

Jacob's father, Joseph Marley, who was himself the son of Thelonius Marley, lived in the coastal community of Portsmouth Common. It was here he toiled in honest and dedicated fashion as a shipbuilder. Though he held a position of no particular note in the history of the place, he made adequate provision for his family. No crest adorned his gate (there was in fact no gate whatsoever), but he provided a middle-class home and often reflected that the fourth-greatest blessing in his life was the roof over his head, the floor under his feet, and the hearth that warmed both of those personal extremities. For the record, as I have given you this much of Joseph, he counted his blessings upward as such: For third, he named the five children who gave life to his home and meaning to his life. For second, Clarissa, who had been his companion, his equal, and his adoration for many years. For first, the One who granted him life.

Into this world, Joseph and Clarissa escorted five young Marleys, from Joseph Jr. to Melinda to William to Alfred to Jacob. To say that any of these were adorned with excess would defame both history and the principles of the family. But, as well, to say they felt want was equally false. They were fed, they were housed, and, indeed, they were loved, all to a point adequate to equip a young man or woman with reasonable armor against the vast and unpredictable battles for the souls of youth.

The hard and successful work of Clarissa and Joseph as parents is worthy to be documented, for of their five, they contributed four balanced and productive citizens of the British Empire. However, our tale is the story of the fifth of Marley. His entire life is not even our concern, though it could be told at some other place. Rather, we search for a particular event, the germination of a seed that, watered by some kind of cupidity, would take root in the pure-hearted young Jacob and find its flower in the deceitful old Marley.

The study of the man must begin with a note about his curious lineage. He was given as his middle name *Thelonius*, which is not an appellation generally worn well by young lads. However, in Jacob's case, his full name was used for far more than a reprimand by his mother. Indeed, he wore the moniker of Jacob Thelonius Marley with pride. For, while not recognized the commonwealth over, in this small region of the family's existence, the name *Thelonius*, spoken, quieted a room, bringing reflection to those who heard it and an unspoken reverence for the deed that had engendered such awe.

Thelonius Marley, father of Joseph, grandfather of Jacob, had worked at so many professions that if a person were to guess at one—say, a butcher—the odds are he most likely would have been right. Had another suggested in surprise that he knew the family and had thought Thelonius was a baker and he was sure others would validate that memory, he too would have been right. It was not that he could not sustain himself in one endeavor. Rather, for men of that time and place endowed with his meager upbringing, simple jobs of limited duration would regularly present themselves, and a worker distinguished himself not so much by what he did as how he was known for doing it. Thelonius labored in a way that was both consistent and admirable. He was known as an honest, hardworking man, and it was his reputation that kept him employed.

Thelonius's life was permanently imprinted with the mark of his character on the evening of January 6, 1734. Up to that point in the winter season, the weather had been good to southern England, mild to the extreme of being almost balmy, and nobody was ungrateful, as it demanded less coal in the hearth and lessened the usual stinging rebuke of the cold on the face every morning and evening. In fact, nobody could be more grateful than St. Crispin's Hall, the old parish workhouse in Portsmouth Common within which those who needed its salvation lived.

A new workhouse had been erected on Warblington Street, St. Crispin's being the original old warehouse donated to the cause. While the intent was to close its doors, and rightfully to tear down the decrepit structure, the great numbers of poor necessitated its remaining open. It barely stood against the winds that so frequently raced off the waters and pelted the little shore village. So a mild winter was indeed a welcome respite.

But sometime between the evening of January fifth and the morning of the sixth, the weather turned. Father Winter visited with a fury and caught up in his belated delivery of seasonal reprimand. The temperatures descended to naught on the scale and the stoves and furnaces of Portsmouth Common roared to greater life. Through the walls of St. Crispin's, so inadequate to brave the change in weather, the cold wind left lines of frost on the inside of all the wooden seams, stitching the wall planks together with a white thread. As the day and then evening wore on, one patron after another would place more fuel in the stove in the main room, unaware that someone just before them had done the same, too impatient to see the effect. As a result, the fire grew hotter and hotter. Sometime after dark, the wall behind the stove gave in to the intense heat and spontaneously combusted in an explosion of flame. Given the position of that partition in the center part of St. Crispin's, the fire spread up through the spine of the building, affecting all rooms within minutes.

By the time Thelonius passed St. Crispin's on the way home from his employment at the chandler's, flames were spreading across the roof. Various residents of the workhouse stood across the street wrapped in whatever clothes they had grabbed as they fled. Thelonius ran to the crowd by the main door where several women were sobbing.

As though his presence were a question asked, a cook turned to him and said, "A shame, a real shame, those children upstairs . . ."

But the end of his sentence dissipated into the frigid air like the steam of an anxious breath, falling on no ears but his own, as Thelonius sprinted into the building and up the stairs. Within a few minutes he emerged, his overcoat bulging. Running to a burly ropemaker who stood mesmerized at the sight of the inferno, Thelonius spread his wool coat to reveal a small child clinging to his waist.

The worker stared in disbelief. "How in the world did you—"

"Take him!" Thelonius yelled. The man quickly

followed the command and grabbed the child as an anxious mother ran to his side to reclaim what she thought she had lost.

Again Thelonius ran into the building. Again he emerged, this time with a soot-covered girl coughing and clasping his neck.

The distraught mothers realized that if any hope could resist the flames, it would come through this newly anointed patron saint. The five remaining women screamed as he came out yet a third time, yelling names and descriptions of their children. Every other man in that small street stood frozen, watching Thelonius with both respect and horror as he turned into the seething hell again. Once more he emerged, and again and again, delivering three more charges to their mothers.

One last woman stood, looking at him imploringly and knowing the gravity of what she asked him with her pleading eyes. She uttered not a word, but grabbed his hand and stared into his face.

He nodded and turned, running into the building that was more flame than wood.

The minutes passed. Some later said they thought they had seen his feet coming down the stairs, visible now through the widening hole that had been the front door.

However, at that moment, St. Crispin's fell in upon itself, folding its walls, its stories, and its lives into an explosion of heat and burning timbers, claiming Thelonius and the final child for whom he had given his life.

It took three days for the remains of the building to cool. When they could walk across the mass, all searched with but one purpose—to find some sign of the child and Thelonius. Finally, beneath the collapsed stairwell, they found their remains, Thelonius's body charred, all earthly beauty gone from the man. Within his coat, the lifeless body of a small boy clung to his waist, unburned where Thelonius had tucked him. The child had died from inhalation, not ten yards from the aching arms of his mother.

In time, the debris was cleared and a new building was erected for some different purpose. To any passerby, it was nondescript and housed some element of Portsmouth Common's shipbuilding economy. However, on the northeast corner, one could find a stone, three up from the ground, with this simple inscription:

THELONIUS
HE GAVE HIS ALL

The reason for this particularly detailed diversion is to make a singular point—Jacob Marley was given his middle name in honor of the grandfather he never knew. Everyone in the southwest of Britain could recite the story, and when the boy was asked his name, his inevitable reply was *Jacob Thelonius Marley*, with an air of substantiating his own character, having claimed the bloodline of the great saver of the children of St. Crispin's.

Jacob found nothing wanting to serve for example and inspiration. Indeed, he carried in the cradle of his name a reminder as his constant companion, a memorial to as good a man as there could be. Yet, it is worthy to note that as the years wore on, Jacob reduced his name to *Jacob T. Marley*, allegedly to narrow the complexity of a simple introduction. In truth, Jacob had grown tired of the explanation of his name for those who did not know of Thelonius, and of the expectations of him from those who did. As he aged, he would shorten his name still further to *Jacob Marley*, leaving the *T* behind him on the shoulder of his particular highway of life. He offered no one an explanation, having no need to justify anything at his station. To himself, he asserted the demand for increased simplicity in the many signatures that were a part of his chosen profession. Yet, deep inside the crusty old miser, he knew that what he hated most was to be reminded of a notion he had taught himself was an unwise transaction—to give too much for too little. The sense of it bothered him, and he expurgated at least part of that from his life by leaving a character in the gutter.

What, then, turned the man? What was so powerful that he discarded that middle name and all that it symbolized? We all ascend or descend in steps, the journey to the high road or the low taken in many increments, the sum total determining our eventual destination. Yet, in the case of Marley, there was a moment, a particular event that transformed Jacob's future and that of all those with whom he would associate.

It occurred in Jacob's youth. It was not negative in its intent, being a circumstance in which the motivation had been to bolster the spirits of the young boy. He was but twelve years of age at the time, and in his course of study of mathematics had demonstrated an unusual comfort with the subject. His instructor had given the class one remarkably difficult problem to decipher. Some gave up; most tried and failed. A very few got the right answer— among them, Jacob. But what particularly caused him to stand out were both the speed with which he did it and the method of derivation he used, showing a maturity in his analytical skills beyond the dozen full seasonal turns he had spent on the earth.

"Jacob," the old schoolmaster had said as he pulled him aside that evening, "I want you to know something. You have a gift, young Jacob. Numbers seem to be a native tongue to you. I urge you to further develop this talent and ready yourself to use the skill in some capacity of service to your fellow man."

Jacob blushed and looked at the ground, stammering out a "thank you." At this one point, the episode might have contributed to Jacob's fulfilling what had been his destiny in life: to take his brilliance with calculation and use it to upgrade the human condition. Indeed, virtuous endeavors great and small awaited his contribution. He would have made *Marley* a household word, in the warmest of terms. Had he but bid thanks and run home to tell his parents, which they always encouraged ("'tis not boasting to tell Mum and Dad!"), he might not have found his way into this story and the one that preceded its telling. It was what happened in the next few seconds that changed the very course of his existence. It would not be an exaggeration to imagine that heaven and hell watched the event, each wrestling for the future of the young man. At this sad moment, some errant germ, a mere fleck of an insidious influence, found its way into the virtuous turn of Marley's earth.

"Young Marley," said the schoolteacher, apparently not having felt he had achieved the desired effect with his compliment, "you are, without a doubt, the single best mathematician I have ever taught."

Of those thirteen words, there was one that held Jacob's attention. He knew them all and had used the sum of them in sentences for many years. But it was the particular arrangement of the thirteen, specifically in the way this one word would betray the other twelve. The word was *best*.

Marley had been no stranger to compliments, having been a boy of greater than average character. He had shown virtues in many areas, which is not to say he did not suffer at times the foibles of youth.

Yet this word, this word! "Best!" Though it seems quite unlikely, Jacob had never thought of his own accomplishments in relation to those of his peers. He had only considered what ought to have been done and whether he did it well. But now he was given a yardstick with which to measure himself against others. And in the first taking of that measure, he was found by this revered teacher to be unequaled. He was the *best*—and he liked it very much.

Do not think he walked out of that school a totally corrupted young man. To the outward eye, he had not changed. But deep within, by reviewing over and over the pleasure that came with those words, he had planted and was starting to cultivate a vine that would in time, from its roots in his ego, reach to entwine and suffocate his very soul.

The warning is given us all that there are seven things which are an abomination to the Lord. One school of thought would suggest that the more of these possessed by one person, the more gnashing there will be at his day of reckoning. However, this makes no account for extreme proficiency in one area. In six of these seven, Marley had no interest, other than the degree to which his one solid vice spilled over into the others. But the seventh—first both in his heart and in the Maker's warning—he had acquired to a level of excellence unrivaled by any man.

It was pride.

Indeed, there is reasonable argument that pride is itself the seedbed of all other sins. Whether that is true or not is perhaps for a different analysis, but certainly Marley's field of pride was a spectacular crop without comparison. This one vice he nurtured to be of more weight than the seven combined in most men, if not seventy times seven.

To tell the whole of Marley's life would be of little value. It took many years for pride to manifest its impact. Indeed, he was at first, after the crucial event, just as he had always been, with far more good than bad in him. But as time went by, the leaves of his deceit began to show. For the next several years, he tried to dress it, conspiring within himself to keep it behind his garden wall. With a practiced behavior, he used the words and actions born of his heart and fostered by his pure nature as a younger man to build a façade of character that covered an increasingly empty soul. As the bootblack covers scuffs, so he polished and repolished his image while sharpening his skills. However the cuts and damages of ill care of the leather could not forever be hidden. In his development, he eventually cast aside the dye and began to nurture what one might think of as the last bit of integrity he possessed—to be who he was.

By the time Jacob was a man, there was never any doubt of his purity. Indeed, no one would debate the complete and total lack of it. He had placed his bushel so firmly and completely upon his light that most would attest the flame was out, the candle melted and sold for its wax, and the darkness a permanent attribute of the hill of Jacob Marley.

Marley forged his path into his financial profession in an ordinary way, apprenticing through all the ordinary roles. What was not ordinary was his skill in the position. Not that he could count better, for how many ways are there to count? A stack of twenty shillings is a pound to any man, no matter how proficient. Jacob's unique trait was in knowing what could be done with those shillings. Where any of his peers could turn a pound into a half crown more, Marley found a way to make it two. He finessed the principles of compounding both his money and his sin as he used this knowledge to build contracts that would stand firm against legal challenge while exacting from his customers more than they had anticipated. The spoken word, to Jacob Marley, was irrelevant. Contract was law, and whatever words needed to be said to get to contract were appropriate if they served that end. While some would call it lying, to Marley, it was simply business. Words would pass from existence in time, whereas contracts would last—in this truth he based his only doctrine, and all his means served this end.

He eventually gained his own clients and, quite to the dismay of his mentor, opened his own countinghouse. He had gained some level of prominence. He lived in London, the only place to do business. He accumulated enough wealth to purchase a home, a rarity. He had found the ideal space, a house built by a Dutch merchant one hundred years prior. Unlike the other homes on this street, it was set back, allowing for a courtyard in front, and assuring Jacob of his privacy from the throngs of the dull and dirty on London's streets. He retained three rooms for himself; the others were let out to businesses, assuring Jacob he would not be bothered by neighbors.

The stair in the entryway was grand. Not that Jacob ever intended to entertain, but occasionally he would meet with a business associate in the parlor, and his ability to negotiate began when the gentleman would gaze in awe at the wide, sweeping staircase and wonder to himself what sort of man of business was successful enough to wander this kind of house.

The only feature that bothered him was in the bedroom. Here, the fireplace had been adorned with tiles, each depicting one of the many familiar stories of the Holy Scriptures. Done in the blue and white delft style of the Dutch artisans, the artwork was superb. In other circumstances this room might have been reserved for a guest room and the commodious hearth would have been an inspiration and conversation piece. But to Marley, who had no guests, each tile called to him, a faint cry from the past when these stories had been the foundation upon which he was raised. He needed none of it! He had found his gift and he was using it and had no room for the introspective condemnation of his ways.

After he took residence in the cold, lonely house, he paid a workman to come and remove the tiles. At first, when the man examined the hearth, he stated that he needed additional tools. When he was due to return, he seemed to conveniently forget the location. Next, when he finally did arrive, he told Marley that the tiles were inset in a way that would ruin the entire fireplace if he tried to remove them. Not accustomed to failure in any endeavor, Marley raised his voice at the worker: "If you are not skilled enough at your trade to remove these infernal tiles, I must find someone who is."

The man did not flinch. He only looked at the hearth and then turned and calmly received the darts of Marley's stare.

"I can remove them, Mr. Marley," he said softly. "What I cannot do is preserve them in the process. Someone far greater than me made these. See here, sir," he went on, as he pointed out the fine points of each picture. "These were done by master craftsmen. There are many imitations today, but they lack the depth of feeling in each image. If these were lost in the removal, I could not redo them."

"I don't want them redone and I don't want them preserved! Of what matter is that?" Marley stammered in frustration and growing anger.

The man waited, his pondering being a function not of wondering what to say, but rather, of giving himself an assurance he said the next thing most correctly. "Once a thing is created, Mr. Marley, I believe it has purpose to it. If I could improve upon these, I would readily remove them. But I cannot. The hand that made these had talents I do not even understand. For me, the loss would be a tragedy, and I fear I would frustrate the intent of their creator."

"You had better leave," Marley ordered.

"Sir, I would also tell you that when these are taken off, with care or with force, you will need to replace all the facing here about. It will be the cost of an entire new fireplace."

Marley was, in the balance, a skinflint. He had accepted many a disagreeable option for the sake of saving a farthing. This was the case with his fireplace, and he finally decided to suffer the daily encounter with Elijah calling fire down on idol worshippers rather than part with any coin.

Time went by and Marley labored. One by one, his parents and siblings abandoned their frustrated pleadings for a relationship. His brothers went on to trades of modest but honest work. None of them achieved any kind of wealth or significance in the worldly sense, but all were happy. This fact annoyed Marley. It was not his own lack of joy in comparison to his siblings that bothered him. It was their total ignorance of their own condition that set his anger afire. They clearly understood nothing about how poor they were. They wasted money on trips to the seashore and children and turkeys at Christmas, and other things for which no investment could be compounded.

His father passed, and Marley could not justify the trip to the funeral, based on the business that demanded his attention. Soon thereafter his mother lay on her deathbed, surrounded by her children, her final words a plea for Jacob's soul. His sister sent him a post upon their mother's passing, telling him of such and imploring him to come to her memorial service. She also asked for his help to secure a decent coffin and place of rest. Marley did cover the cost of the funeral and the coffin and the plot and the flowers.

"Melinda," he wrote simply, "I have given to this messenger all the funds required to properly lay our mother to rest. Should there be any extra, you and the others may split it equally, or unequally, as you decide."

In reading this, Melinda's heart rejoiced. Perhaps an angel had shown compassion for Clarissa's appeal in Jacob's behalf and there would be a chance to redeem her brother back from the darkness in which he lived. However, her brief cause for hope was dashed as quickly as it came.

"In return for this, I ask one thing of you and our brothers. I am a busy man. I have no time for frivolities. I request that none of you attempt to contact me again. We are all adults and must make our own ways in the world. Should you not possess the industry, thrift, or intelligence to cover your expenses in this life, that is your pit into which you have dug yourself and one you must climb out of on your own, or be content to lie within. Family gatherings to me are a nuisance [which was an odd observation, given that Marley had never attended one] and of no contribution to my condition. I take my leave of you, and wish you would do so of me as well. Signed, J. Marley."

Though his family members honored his request, they mourned. No communiqué was ever offered again.

Melinda and her brothers carried Jacob's absence as a weight upon their hearts for the rest of their lives, a sorrowful corner of their otherwise happy existence. In visits with one another, they occasionally spoke of Jacob in hushed tones and offered prayers in his behalf. "Uncle Jacob" was no more than a figment of the imagination to their children, a character from a book who came to life only in the exaggerated tales they told one another of his evil ways.

Marley, however, once he had sealed the note and handed it to the courier, never thought of them again.

He had no friends, only acquaintances built in the course of business. There were no women in his life. There was not sufficient recompense in such a relationship to justify it.

So Marley went his way in the world, confining himself to the narrow environment of the Exchange, his countinghouse, and his investments. With each entry in his ledgers, his purse became richer, and the rut of his life deeper.

He was indeed an unpleasant man, wearing his greed in his countenance. Those with a shred of goodness in them went to any length to avoid him. Even those aligned with Marley in their self-absorbed version of morality despised him, for he turned their common iniquity against them. As necessary to conduct a deal, they wore a mask of pleasantries to spend time with him, convincing neither themselves that they were fooling him, nor him that they meant any of it.

One particular specialty of Marley and his counting-house was that of rent assessment for his clients. Though landlords were terrified of him, they saw in his compassion-less dedication to collections a means to assure their own income, and enjoyed the benefit while remaining at arm's length from his heartless deeds. Thus, he built quite a port-folio of properties. It was said that when delinquent tenants saw Marley's carriage approaching, they simply began to pack. Most of the properties were closer to dereliction than quaintness. Marley found the lessees of these residences to be the worst payers, a condition he had turned to his ad-vantage. When someone fell behind on their payments, he would negotiate a division with the owner, keeping for him-self the greater portion of what he could collect rather than the standard percentage he was normally allowed in the contracts. Accustomed to getting nothing at all from des-perate tenants, his clients took the deal as readily as Marley took them.

One particularly cold and dreary February day, Marley

settled in his carriage to travel to Camden Town. His errand was to settle the negligent debt of a young couple in one of the properties he managed. Here, in a small, modest apartment, they had settled just after their marriage two years prior. For twenty-one months, they had been timely in their payments. But at that time, industrialization in the factory had eliminated the man's position. They had paid in full that month, but their payments had diminished in amount in the subsequent two periods, each time with a promise that they would make up the difference in the following payment with a new job the husband would surely secure. Marley let them stay those two months, but not because he believed a word they said. He had seen this many times before. People would sell all they had to pay their rent. He allowed them enough time not to find a job but rather to liquidate all their assets, realizing all he possibly could from their dwindling resources until they had exhausted their funds. Sensing when that moment occurred had become an art form, and Marley was its grand master. This was that day, and he swooped in for his kill.

As he arrived, he walked stiffly to the door, rapped twice, waited as long as he felt he should—about five seconds—and then rapped again. He knew they knew he was coming.

The door opened slowly and only partway, as if the narrowed entrance might keep out the message from this unwelcome visitor. With a practiced regimen, Marley tipped his hat in deference to protocol rather than to respect and, at the same time, placed his foot next to the doorjamb. After multiple experiences with this marking of territory, he had begun having all his boots made with reinforced sides and soles to brace his foot against the likely response.

This time, the door did not slam. Instead, from around the edge of the border between warmth and cold, home and homelessness, life and death, a somber man appeared, ramrod straight in his posture. He was neither friendly nor resentful. He was weary.

"Mr. Marley," he said as he lowered his head in the slightest nod.

"Mr. Cummings," Marley said perfunctorily. "You know why I am here."

"I do," the man replied softly. He looked past Marley at the light snow being whipped into small ice-darts by the persistent wind. "Come in."

Marley did not want to come in. He wanted to tell them to leave, handing them their eviction notice to make it official, and then depart. He had showed up in person, rather than mailing the document, only because he found it hastened any court deliberations should he be challenged. Everything needed to show a return, and that was the yield afforded him by taking half a day in the cold to deliver his ominous order.

"I am quite fine here. I want to inform you that due to your late and insufficient payments—"

"Mr. Marley," the man said so gently that even though it was an interruption, it sounded as though Marley had given way in his speech for the comment. "I ask you in to try to keep the warmth in the home for my wife's sake. Please, may we talk inside?"

Ah, Marley thought. *His wife's sake.* Should he continue to stand outside, and the man present that his wife was swollen with some dreaded illness, Marley's coldness both in his spirit and in that which he allowed in the home might be held against his case, tying up the disposition of this home for weeks.

Rather than reply, he stepped in, registering his dissatisfaction with the request by bumping Cummings as he shuffled past him.

When the door shut, Cummings turned, and Marley picked up where he had left off.

"—it is necessary to have you vacate the home, as you have forfeited on your contract."

Marley stuck out his hand from the folds of his coat and presented an envelope, sealed with a wax stamp. "Here is the eviction notice. You are to be out by end of day today. You may take your possessions, but if you wish to leave them, you will be assessed—"

"Mr. Marley," Cummings said with some alarm, "I know that we have not met our obligations and that we are due our consequences, but my wife . . ." His voice trailed off as he gestured to the chair by the table, where, unnoticed up to this point by Marley, sat the most pregnant woman he had ever seen. She was indeed swollen, and, to Marley's perspective, it was with an illness. It was the malady contracted by so many newlyweds that, in love or foul misjudgment, yields the sickness of noise, discomfort, unnecessary expense, and trouble. Marley was no fool. He knew the race depended upon the continued addition of new generations, but what a bothersome, inconvenient way to bring them into the world! And, it seemed to him, most couples selected the most inopportune time financially to take on this investment burden that would never repay them.

"Mr. Marley," Cummings continued, "my wife is in no condition to pack our things and even worse to find herself in the cold. She is but one or two weeks from bearing our baby, maybe even less." He looked at her with concern, then back at Marley with pleading in his eyes. "We need only a month; we can find arrangements when we have gotten a week past the birth. She is proud and has not wanted to share our condition with her family. But I believe she will now reconsider. I give you my word we will be out thirty days from now."

Marley felt his rage rise within him. He shook the letter at the couple. "Your word. Your word," he said slowly, trying to draw out the phrase in disgust. "This envelope is the evidence of how you keep your word! And her pride! So, I must bear the loss in the selfish display of her pride? I would suggest that a little humility is long overdue at this point. Do not make me to suffer at the sin of her pride!"

"But, Mr. Marley, you know my position was eliminated—"

"None of my affair," Marley said brusquely. "I have no interest in your personal business. You made a contract with me. I kept up my end of it. You did not. You forfeited, per the language of the agreement. In fact, if you read it carefully, you will see I have already given you two extra days."

"Two days, Mr. Marley, is appreciated, but is not enough. She is so fragile. This pregnancy has been long in coming and difficult in its progression. I fear for her health and our baby's."

Marley's eyes narrowed to slits as he glared at Cummings. "Fears you should have considered when you decided to have a child. Surely the term of a pregnancy was no surprise to you—a simple calculation would have told you that this baby would be here in the cold of February. You made either a bad choice or no choice—both of which you, not I, are responsible to resolve."

"But sir, I did not choose to change the factory, to put in the machines that did our work. I was employed well—you even said so when we signed the agreement. It was not—"

"Enough!" barked Marley. "There is no end to this discussion that will lead to any outcome other than one of two options. The first is your producing all your back payments and, according to the agreement in the case of late arrangements, paying two months forward for my security; the second is your being out by the end of today. I trust you do not have the payments?" he asked with a sarcastic sneer.

With that, the room was silent. Marley had avoided the gaze of the pregnant wife. She slowly stood, and the movement caught him off guard, causing him now to reactively turn and look in her direction. As he met her eyes, he knew through his years of managing the affairs of the indolent what he would see. There would be tears, pleading in her face. Nothing but manipulative emotions designed to separate Marley from the fixed and appropriate outcome of his settlement.

However, he was surprised. This woman was not crying, and she most certainly was not afraid of Marley, or, he surmised, of anything. She held her protruding belly beneath one hand as she walked toward Marley, never releasing his stare.

Marley too was afraid of nothing, and though this moment made him uncomfortable, he refused to back away as she drew closer. When she came within a yard of Marley, she stopped and, with her other hand, reached behind her neck and unfastened a thin gold chain. Without ever moving her eyes, she held the necklace up between their faces. From it was suspended a single pearl, small but brilliant. Marley was momentarily startled as its translucence almost seemed to draw in light from the woman and reflect it outward.

"If I give you this, how many additional months would it buy us?" she asked with a firm defiance.

How an average woman such as this had come into possession of a gem this remarkable was beyond his imagination. Swiftly and silently he assayed the value of the tribute, deliberately stifling his facial expression from displaying his impression. He calculated the most conservative price the piece would command, most likely far below what he would be able to gain in negotiations. He calculated that in rent, and then halved that number of days. Then he halved it again. And again, and again. Finally, he halved it one more time.

"Three days," he replied coldly, never releasing her gaze and never raising a hand toward the pearl.

Cummings gasped, knowing that the value of the necklace was far more than a fraction of a month's rent. But his wife did not waver in her stare, or in her suspension of the necklace in Marley's line of sight.

"So be it, then—take it!" She did not move one inch to make it easier for Marley to grasp the necklace. With an only slightly perceptible regret in her voice, she said, "It was a gift from my brother."

Marley did not miss that minute fluctuation. *Weakling*, he thought. For a moment, he had actually admired her resolve.

He reached up and took the necklace, placing it in his

coat pocket. With that, he removed a watch and, looking at it, said, "It is a quarter to two. At a quarter to two on Thursday, you need to be out. I will be here at that time. If you are not gone, I will return at a quarter past two with the constable. He will deal with you appropriately."

He tipped his hat incongruously to the couple he had just condemned, and then he stepped out into the cold.

As he walked to his carriage, he heard not a sound from the house—no wailing, no curses. Of course, had there been any, he would not have paid them any attention. He was oblivious to all such: the emotions, the pain, the concern. Oblivious to the final plea implicit in the simple comment that "it was a gift from my brother." Rather, he was rapidly calculating his gain on the necklace.

At twenty minutes before two on Thursday, Marley's carriage worked its way across the cobblestones to what, in five minutes' time, would be the previous home of the Cummings family. A loaded cart stood by the door, the husband emerging with a last item to be placed on the meager pile of their possessions.

The carriage driver leapt down, opened the door for Marley, and placed a step beneath it to help him out into the raw wind and driving mixture of sleet and snow.

Marley stepped into the apartment, followed by Mr. Cummings, tipped his hat in the slightest possible manner, and then began speaking without bothering to look at the couple.

"I will inspect the house. Any damage done, filth left, or inconvenience created by remaining possessions will result in assessments. You will pay me before departing. Do you understand?"

Mr. Cummings gently said to Marley, "I assure you, Mr. Marley, there is no damage, what little we have is gone, and the home is clean."

His wife walked up to Marley and, with a steady voice and fire in her eyes, said, "Cleaner by a great deal more than when we moved in."

Marley looked back at her and then mumbled, "Good. As it should be." Then, turning to the man, he said, "Nonetheless, I will inspect it and notify you if I see a problem. Wait here."

He left the couple standing in the entryway as he surveyed the home. His practiced eye made quick work of the environment, knowing what problems typically were created and, of those, which ones he would levy the greatest penalty for. He was frustrated to find nothing.

"All right, then," he said. "Out and be gone with you!"

The threesome stepped out into the cold, dreary storm. Marley watched as the woman took her place between the pull shafts to help her husband haul the small collection of their things to who knew where. Her husband gently took her hands off the rails, kissed her on the cheek, and then lifted her to sit on the front of the cargo box in a spot that he had obviously prepared for her.

"Fool," Marley muttered. "Doesn't he even understand that putting her there will make his job harder?"

Cummings put a harness around his shoulders and lifted the handles. Then, straining against the weight, the resistance on the wheels from the ruts of frozen snow, and the thousand stings of the driving weather, he pulled.

Marley began walking back to his carriage.

There are times in our lives when we remember things for no known purpose, the memory sitting in our pocket like a lonely button fallen from some unknown garment that we save in the anticipation of one day having a flash of inspiration, "This belongs to my old black coat!" For some reason, this day, Marley heard in the back of his mind the departing words of the Cummingses, and they stuck with him.

"John, will you be all right?"

"Sure, I am good enough. Hold tight so you don't fall, Fan. Here we go."

It was of so little consequence at that moment that, although he took note of it as he put his hand on the carriage door, he had forgotten about it by the time he was seated. Raising his voice, he rudely commanded his driver to hasten back to his office.

Later that day, Marley sat quite still at his desk. His elbow rested upon the broad surface as he dangled the pearl necklace in front of him. Several times in the last hour, he had concluded to visit his favorite precious stones dealer and sell the pearl. It should be pointed out, so as not to mislead anyone with regard to Marley having a favorite anything, that this man was just so approbated not because he was particularly good at his trade, and certainly not because Marley cared for him, but in reality because he was most likely to succumb to Marley's withering protestations in a negotiation.

Yet, each time he would make an effort to push his chair back and rise to the task, he paused, bumping into some force of uncertainty he could not quantify. The market was good enough, he had the time this afternoon, and he certainly would have liked to dispose of any reference to this strong-willed woman who had left him so unsettled. But he could not move. Thus repelled, he stared now at the little innocent gem, attempting to draw from its luster a cause for the hesitation, as though it might surrender some reason to his practiced gaze. No insight revealed itself.

Finally, he yielded. Marley opened the writing tray in his desk. It was particularly thick, but should someone remove it from its rollers, he would find it to be surprisingly light. Marley triggered a small clasp on its underbelly and lifted out the inside of the drawer, revealing a shallow but secure and secret compartment nested in what should have been solid wood. Therein lay a few papers, a key, and some other items Marley did not want to deposit in the usual places. He took a blank ledger page and folded it into an envelope around the pearl necklace, pushed it to the back of the compartment, and shut the top.

"In time," he said aloud to himself.

3

A little more than a month later, Marley was again at the home from which he had forced the Cummings couple. As was his custom, he had personally collected the first month's rent payment from the new occupants. He had raised their rate just after they moved in, citing his right to do so annually in the agreement, and rehearsed the covenants they had agreed to. As he began his journey back to the countinghouse, he quickly found the progress of his carriage slowed to a walk. He reached up and banged on the ceiling with his fist, just below the seat of his driver.

"Move on, man. I have to be back at work, not touring London."

His driver leaned over and spoke in an exaggerated whisper, "We are quite stuck, sir—it is a funeral procession."

Marley growled and opened the side curtain of his carriage. He was a sudden and unwilling participant in the midst of a crowd of walkers paying respects to someone being inconveniently drawn in a box up ahead. He looked at the man next to him, who kept an even pace with his slow-moving carriage.

"You, sir, are you part of this?"

The man looked up soberly. He was young but well dressed, an obvious man of business, Marley thought.

"I am, sir."

"How long will this drag out?"

"We are going to St. Dunstan's."

"Good heavens," Marley muttered. Rapping again on the ceiling, he yelled, "They are going to St. Dunstan's; find another way." However, they were quite surrounded by mourners, and, try as he might, the driver could not extricate the carriage from the throng.

Marley leaned out and looked disapprovingly through the quiet, shuffling crowd at the simple hearse ahead of them.

Without glancing at the man next to him, he said, "You knew this one?"

The man looked up at Marley again. "I do. She was my sister."

"Hmmm" was all Marley could offer as a condolence.

After an awkward silence, Marley observed, "You are young," curious about the man's fine appearance.

"Not as young as she," he replied.

Quiet again.

"Cholera?" Marley asked, momentarily fearful of breathing in the wake of air from the procession, though he would know, if he thought about it, that it posed no threat to him through those means.

"No, in fact, it was the cold." The man paused in his reply, seeming to have difficulty with what he was about to say. "Apparently, she lived on the street, and this weather that just passed took her."

"Hmmm" again. "Just as well. Decreases the surplus population."

The man looked at Marley with an offended expression. "Pardon me, sir!"

Marley waved his hand. "Malthus. Don't suppose you've read him," he said disparagingly. "Says the population is growing faster than our food supply. A little weaning of the weaker stock would benefit us all." He paused. "In many ways."

"I've read it," the other offered. "Whatever the truth of it, this one," nodding his head toward the coffin, "this one was not surplus. She was . . ." his voice trailed off as he visibly steeled himself against some emotion. Then he touched his hat as if to put an end to it and said, "No mind, not your business."

"Well," Marley said, not letting go of the critique, "there's always a cause. Perhaps her husband was incapable of applying himself to hard work. Who knows with the poor?"

The man continued to look forward, staring at the hearse. "Of him I know little. You could be right. She didn't come to me when they could not meet their needs, so I have no idea what condition put them there."

Marley wondered aloud, "Why not the poorhouse? They make arrangements for those not willing to support themselves."

The walker changed his tone. "That, sir, is another discussion," he said condescendingly. "I am quite tired of supporting those institutions, when apparently they don't even seem to function well enough. If they did, she would not have been subjected to the elements."

Marley looked back at the man. "I agree! I too find that far too great a percent of my taxes goes toward supporting the indolent. Free housing! Free food! No wonder they don't go out and work. With all the comforts, they are inclined to just live upon our generosity rather than their own industry."

The other man nodded his head in agreement.

Marley changed the subject. He did not care to make small talk, but occasionally he used it to get at information he desired. "You are dressed well to be walking from Camden Town. What is it you do?"

"Oh, I don't live there. She did. I am a financier. I work at Pembroke's."

"The countinghouse?"

"The same."

They proceeded quietly for another minute.

Marley had a thought. A thought that was yet another confluence of the strands of his life, bundled together in one knot. Had he but let it pass, the course he would follow would have been drastically different. Yet, while Marley possessed an uncanny ability to reconcile numbers, he had long ago suppressed the greater gift of listening to his conscience. What faint voice it still had was trying to urge him to end the conversation, to sit upon his thought, to mentally move on to some other, any other distraction. Even his driver saw a small break in the crowd he might have taken, a break offered by an unseen force attempting to help them avoid what would come next, but in a moment of indecision the driver let it close again, leaving both men at this crossroads of character.

Marley tried to seem casual as he spoke next. "Pembroke's," he said, "is a good house. But old Pembroke himself, he is not a forward-thinking man. I also operate a countinghouse. It is growing, and I need to extend my efforts. Should you be interested in discussing employment, perhaps through an apprenticeship, after I find out something of your background and training, I would suggest you call at my offices a fortnight from today. At one." Marley paused, and then donned his crusty, threatening countenance. "Should you have no interest in that capacity, do not plan on coming and wasting my time petitioning me about any other subject. I am a busy man."

The man looked at him, his expression unruffled. "I might come. Your name?"

"Marley, Jacob Marley. Yours?"

"Ebenezer Scrooge. I will give it some thought."

With that, Marley's driver apparently found an escape, less opportune than the previous one, made open by other regions that now provided this gap. Carelessly bumping several in the procession, he broke free and hurried the carriage down a side street.

Two weeks from that moment, indeed, as the clock tower completed its prelude to the chime of 1:00 p.m., the door handle to Jacob Marley's countinghouse turned, and, in complete synchronicity with the peal of the bell, in walked Ebenezer Scrooge. A balding clerk, peering over spectacles perched on the bridge of his nose, turned in perfect harmony to the close of the door. With no greeting, he stated rather than asked, "You are Mr. Marley's 1:00 p.m. appointment. He will appreciate your timeliness. He has no more than twenty minutes. You are . . . ?"

"Ebenezer Scrooge." He offered it plainly, with no fanfare, with no friendliness. It was a business transaction in itself.

"You may be seated while I notify him."

Scrooge took the clerk aback as he quickly and defiantly stated, "I will not. I would appreciate if Mr. Marley would return my commitment to timeliness by beginning this discussion at our appointed hour. If there is time to sit and wait, then there is no time for me to be here."

The clerk, whose name was Duffin, was clearly not accustomed to this type of visitor. Working for Jacob Marley had hardened him against most brusque interactions, but Scrooge was a different sort. Duffin attempted to hide his nervousness behind a wall of protocol. He opened the door to an office in the back and spoke to its occupant. When he turned to Scrooge to say, "You may come in," Scrooge had already brushed by him.

Marley was entering a cipher upon some ledger that no doubt was the accounting of someone's life as expressed through the sole lens of the person's debits, credits, and timeliness of each. It was an attempt on Marley's part to make an early and subtle statement of his own importance relative to his visitor's. No stranger to the tactic, nor victim of it in his past, Scrooge took a chair and began to speak.

"Mr. Marley, I am employed as a junior accountant. As such, I am paid thirty shillings per week, and with my current work schedule of approximately ten hours each and every day, that amounts to sixpence per hour. In the course of my work, I have saved my employer nearly 360 pounds over the prior nine months of my engagement. If you were to perform the calculation, you would know that I am producing a net increase to my employer of thirty shillings per hour. Every minute that you sit here furthering your business, you cost my business 600 percent growth on my investment. If the net result of your interest in my employment is not worth your discontinuing your work, I suggest that I consider this cost of my time a loss and do my best to diminish its relative impact by leaving."

While Marley did not look up during this mathematical oration, as was his nature, he made the calculations in his mind as Scrooge lectured him. Following closely and with precision, he placed his quill firmly in its base the moment Scrooge sounded the apparent finale, adding his own rendition to the accounting.

"And, if you were my apprentice, I should gather you would work for no less, and would wish more. Assume I pay you 10 percent more. Certainly I would settle for no less net gain to my business than your current employer, and therefore if your pay was increased by 10 percent, so your contribution should be by at least as much. That would make a total increase to my assets of more than 4,700 pounds per year. Why don't we discuss to what approach you would attribute your ability to accomplish that?"

Scrooge stared unflinchingly at Marley and said with vitriol, "I am not here to be your apprentice. I am here to be your partner. My current employer is adequate, though admittedly not as successful on the whole as your countinghouse. You should note that the contribution from my field of responsibility at Pembroke's would actually outperform your establishment. I should be partner there soon enough. With time I will assist my employer to move on to his well-deserved and far-overdue retirement, and therefore there must be a reason for me to leave at this time. That would be to become partner now." He sat silently, unmoved and unshaken.

Marley reacted poorly. "You, sir, are impertinent to come in here and tell me of what status I should make your employ—"

"Oh, please," Scrooge dismissed his anger. "Impertinence is a complaint against inefficient social convention. I am competent beyond my years and intend not to waste any time having you guess as to that fact or wait to observe it yourself via experience. We are here to conduct business. Money and time are my business, not pleasantries. If you cannot see the value of a partnership, let us be done with this quickly."

With that Scrooge stood and began wrapping his muffler around his neck. "Good day, Mr. Marley."

Marley continued as though he did not see Scrooge make a move to leave. "Mr. Scrooge, I have no question as to your competence in your own mind. However, I would fire myself for my own carelessness were I not assured of such a fact in mine."

"And how do you propose to comfort your sense of it?" Scrooge said, showing neither increased interest by removing the muffler or an increased threat by leaving.

"Provide me with a record of your best accounts—and your worst—and allow me to see the management of your investments. Though I am sure your employer would be uncomfortable with my looking at his books, I have no intent to petition his business. However, I am not going to risk mine without evidence of what you can do."

Scrooge responded quickly. "I will collect the books and leave them with you this evening at seven o'clock. I will pick them up at a quarter to eight tomorrow morning. If you are interested, tell me at that time."

With that, and without any closing comments or even an empty but customary offering of "adieu," Scrooge turned and left. Duffin looked up to provide a terse good-bye, but Scrooge walked by without acknowledging him.

Marley looked respectfully after him. He was not sure he had ever met anyone who cut so efficiently through the useless chatter and noise of dialogue to get to the real business of business. Although Scrooge was younger than

Marley—by at least fifteen years, as he sized him up—he seemed to have learned the edge that makes someone a good man of the trade.

The books were dropped off as promised, at the minute they were promised, and Marley spent the evening before the old fireplace studying each ledger in detail, making notes on his observations.

In the morning, Scrooge walked into the counting-house to find Marley sitting at his desk, books precisely where he had set them the evening before.

"It does not appear you even looked at them," Scrooge said with disgust as he collected the journals into his leather valise.

"Mr. Scrooge," Marley responded coldly, "I said I would look at them and I did. I do what I say—always—and I do not take kindly to implications that I do differently."

Scrooge stopped closing his bag and stood, expressionless, staring at Marley.

"I have questions about your accounts. There will be no partnership unless my concerns are addressed. Yet you seem ready to leave. I take it you give me the options only of declining a potential business arrangement or accepting one on no more than your desire to have it. There is no balance in that contract, and I will have none of it."

"I need to be at my duties by eight sharp."

"Ah, a further testament to my point. You were either careless in not allowing for time for me to investigate these details, in which case we have nothing to discuss, or you purposefully did not allow time as a strategy, in which case we have nothing to discuss."

Scrooge glared at Marley. "There is nothing wrong with my accounts, and you know it as well as I. They are flawlessly in order—"

"Oh, but I agree they are in perfect order. They must be! The entries I found demonstrate a man more concerned with the accuracy of his entries than the value of them, else you would not have recorded for time and memorial your failures."

Never removing his eyes from Marley's, Scrooge reached into the bag now slung about his shoulders and removed the journals, tossing them on Marley's desk in a manner designed to create the largest slap possible when they hit the wood. In the next room, Duffin leapt from his chair at the sound, calling out, "Is everything all right, sir?"

Scrooge said through clenched teeth, "What failures?" It was not a question but a dare to extrapolate from the books one cipher of evidence of error.

"Let's begin with Higbee," Marley said, obviously prepared. "You allowed him three months without payment, then repossessed the item—what was it, a ring, I believe?—then made an entry selling it for but a tenth of what it was worth."

It was a statement, but Marley let it hang there as exhibit one in this surreptitious trial of Scrooge.

Scrooge responded immediately, as though he were prepared for that exact question. "If you look at the dates, you will notice that the first missed payment was in April of '07. Should you bother to consult your memory—"

"Gold was at a three-year low on the Exchange. I am more aware of it than I wish."

"Yes. Good. This account was not my doing initially, but I took it on when I joined the firm. Higbee was not altogether destitute, though completely irresponsible, and his earnings had kept a slightly better pace than his expenditures. I determined that although my predecessor had done a poor job securing collateral, I would be able to 'arrange,'" he said it with some special emphasis, "to channel some of his other assets into collateral for the loan. Had I closed the agreement on him at that point, the ring would have been resold for a fraction of its price."

"And yet, three months later, that is exactly what happened."

"Yes. The price of gold did not respond to the changes in economy, and Mr. Higbee's other debtors were first in line to claim his assets when he became bankrupt. Thus, I was left with nothing but the ring to resolve the account."

"A poor decision, don't you think, Mr. Scrooge?"

"A risk, Mr. Marley. This business is about risk. My net performance is outstanding. Nobody performs without some risks not paying."

"And what is it you think you risked?"

Looking genuinely confused, Scrooge said, "Why, the value of the loan against the ring."

"No!" Marley said and slammed his fist against the desk. "No, man! That was but a farthing in the pound of your risk. Your risk was your reputation. This man Higbee, I am sure, is like all the other weak, selfish, ne'er-do-well dregs that chain down our economy. England's ship of state would sail with greater speed were it not pulling along the anchors of the careless and dishonest who do not settle their obligations. I am sure he talks. Talks to all his friends, equally matched in their ethics and resolve, and what does he say? 'Oh, that Scrooge,' he mocks. 'He's a soft one. Agree to anything he says because when push comes to shove, he will relent.' And one says it to another to another, and you are flush with pride as they line up at your door, only to suck the blood out of your accounts like so many ticks attached to your ankles."

Scrooge nodded slowly. "I agree. That is why I supplied the information to assure Mr. Higbee's eventual interment in debtor's prison, where, to my understanding, he still resides. I agree with your assessment of the risk, and let me assure you, I realized the loss could have been avoided. It was with that regret that I wanted to hang Higbee publicly for others to see. I am sure you found no other such losses in my books from that point forward."

"I did not—a few prior, but none since. Yet, Mr. Scrooge, there is no room for regret. It is a poor return. It is the character of this level of society to not consider the future. No, the opportunity was to collect on Higbee at the first missed payment! There is only the here and the now. No future. No consequence that can rescript the past. It is written, and all its miserable, 'regrettable' decisions must hang with you and you with them."

There was a brief silence between them. Old Scrooge,

who was not old at all but whose demeanor had made him old, determined that never would Marley or any man be able to point out a weakness in him again. He would avoid even the appearance of mercy. He would give no ground whatsoever. He would settle all accounts as written. He would forge a greater, stronger business than Marley.

"One other thing," Marley said, breaking the silence. "Are you married?"

It was an odd question from Scrooge's perspective, odd in its placement in the conversation, and odd in its timing in his life.

"No . . ."

"Good," Marley said.

"But I am engaged," Scrooge concluded.

Marley looked up with obvious displeasure. "Since you are not yet married, tell me, where is the value in it? Oh, I realize there are certain benefits—cooked meals, clean laundry, an orderly home—but all these things can be hired out. At the end of the day, a wife demands that you leave the responsibilities of business that keep her in such good circumstances and hurry home to play with children or attend to her supposed needs, when her station in life would improve if she left you to develop your accounts. She does not see, for some reason that befuddles me, what an unrelenting master is poverty. There is nothing so hard upon the total state of man and society. And yet, as we attempt to resolve this poverty by avoiding the problem in the first place with the fruits of our industry and thrift, we are condemned for seeking to create wealth. I say, it is not just."

Marley continued, "And this horrific decision is made over and over again for what reason?" He answered his own question, seeming to have difficulty even saying the words. "In the name of love. Love is perhaps the poorest of all investments."

"I was young and," Scrooge paused for a moment, "'heady' when we were engaged. I thought not of greater things at that time." He seemed quite off balance in the face of Marley's assault on marriage.

"Yes, but you are not young now, or at least, not as young as you were. You say you are betrothed, not married. If you now have a more worldly vision, why do you stay as such?"

Scrooge just stared at him. Marley knew he had opened a crack, had challenged Scrooge's commitment with intellect. The cuts in the tree had been made, and gravity was prepared to do its work. Marley gave the trunk a push.

"It is your business, of course, as long as it does not interfere with this partnership. But since you still have a choice, I urge you, man, rethink this decision. If you had to choose today, if there were no agreement with her, would you make this one?"

Scrooge was thinking about the Higbee ring. The one he had purchased from his own accounts for 10 percent of its value. The one that now marked his supposed commitment to his fiancée, Belle. She had been thrilled to receive that ring, though it had been years earlier. It would break her heart, he thought, to remove it from her finger. Yet Marley was correct. His associates, always saying such things as "have to get home to the missus," terminated their days earlier than necessary. He loved Belle—or at least, he *had* loved Belle. He had not thought much on love these last few years, though Belle was with him constantly. He supposed he did still love her, given that nothing had signaled a change, but there was no question that his relationship with Belle did not occupy his thoughts the way it had when they were younger.

"I will consider it," he said quietly.

Marley repeated, "As I said, your business." Then, looking sternly at Scrooge, he said, "Just don't make it my business by letting it affect this firm."

And so the partnership of Marley and Scrooge was born. Those accustomed to passing by the firm's old sign might say, "Not 'Marley and Scrooge,' but 'Scrooge and Marley.' I know that sign—I have walked beneath it for many seasons and I am quite sure of those old letters." And they would be right. The sign that hung over the doings of these two for so many years, and over Scrooge after Marley's death, did in fact say "Scrooge and Marley." That was not, however, what it was supposed to be.

In the early weeks of their partnership, Jacob Marley gave Ebenezer Scrooge the assignment of handling the legalities of the name change. Marley saw no need for altering the name from "Jacob Marley," but Scrooge countered that if each of them had to find and manage his own accounts, then Scrooge's importance in the firm needed to be of public affirmation. Marley reluctantly agreed and thought nothing of it again until a week later when, coming to his office, he saw the workmen erecting the sign with Scrooge's name in the first order.

"Ebenezer!" he yelled as he walked into the office. Finding his new partner at the second desk that had been installed in the countinghouse, he said, "The sign is wrong. Did you arrange this?"

Scrooge looked up slowly after completing the trans-action he was studying. "I did."

"This was not our agreement."

"Our agreement was that we would use both our names as the name of the business."

"Our agreement was that the firm would be 'Marley and Scrooge.'"

"No, Jacob, our agreement was that we would use both our names. 'Marley and Scrooge' was offered merely as an example of what that might be."

Marley knew that had not been the intent. He also knew—knew better, in fact—that intent had no place in business negotiations. There was no documentation, no signature on intent. Words, as we have said, meant very little to Jacob. It was all in the contract, and in this case, the contract was not there.

"I will redo the arrangements if you wish," Scrooge offered thinly, suggesting the cost of such a change. Marley was, of course, perturbed at this younger version of himself. And of the fact that Scrooge was exactly that younger version, Marley was admiring as well, the way an opponent who had just been checkmated might feel about the one who possessed the skill to do it to him.

And so it stood. "Scrooge and Marley" went up over the door.

They began their arrangements with an agreement (written, in triplicate), that each man would retain nine-tenths of his gain achieved in every transaction, passing one-tenth to the other. In time, Marley assured, that split would move to 80/20, then 70/30, and so forth. However, the men found that they quickly balanced each other out and would share responsibilities on every arrangement. They both hated dealing with people, but Marley was more practiced and accepting of the necessity of it to keep the business moving, so he took on most of those duties. Scrooge, on the other hand, was more creative, and would examine new business opportunities that had no precedent in the firm, finding those in which they could subtly and effectively choke their clients to release more than they reasonably would have, were all sides known. Thus, they quickly came to an agreement that they would split all proceeds 50/50. This had little to do with any idea of fairness, or of give and take. Rather it was done for practicality's sake, born of the profound, deep, and resolute distrust they had for one another. It was the perfect counterweight to the traits that would make them otherwise incompatible.

Scrooge's first contributions to the business were to move most of his clients from Pembroke's firm to Scrooge and Marley. Pembroke was infuriated, and said as much at the Exchange in as public a setting as he could find. But he was a trusting soul and had not secured agreements from his apprentices that would prohibit them from contacting their former clients. Within a few months, Scrooge and Marley had one fewer competitor.

Not more than weeks past the establishment of their partnership, Scrooge was summoned by Belle to visit with her in her parents' home. Though Scrooge had not yet suggested they terminate their relationship, his heart and spirit had done so, and Belle clearly heard their ominous pronouncement. For you see, one cannot betray oneself. Scrooge's heart had left Belle. Even before he had formed his partnership with Marley, he had been slowly retreating from his commitment. Marley's views on marriage had not initiated the demise of the relationship, nor had they placed the final coffin nail, but they had gone a great distance toward making the funeral arrangements.

At this time, Belle said what Scrooge would not, that he had placed their relationship on the scale in the countinghouse and found that it would not balance. Their engagement had come up short in its books.

She handed Scrooge the ring and bade farewell to him and their bond. Scrooge knew his heart ached, but he had encased it so firmly in the resolve of business that he did not allow it to work its softening agents on his soul. It surrendered, ceasing to try to wake the man from his determined journey.

He took the ring and placed it in his cash box in the office. Scrooge knew its worth, and oftentimes he calculated his potential return if he were to sell it in the healthier gold markets, but for some reason, he could not. He kept it secreted in the velvet-lined bottom of the cold, metal tomb, away from Marley and away from his own view, not ten feet from Marley's secret drawer in which a solitary pearl necklace lay. Each man kept hidden from the other, and as much as possible from his own conscience, the one true testament to his life that refused to be released.

There are stories to be told of all the years of Scrooge and Marley, but the plot of each is identical. Identical to how Fan and her husband were treated, identical to the way in which the firm became Scrooge and Marley rather than Marley and Scrooge, identical to why the pearl was still in Marley's drawer and why Scrooge's returned engagement ring sat in his. To tell one is to tell them all. There was a monotony of greed that laced every day, a monotony that both Marley and Scrooge worshipped as their assets grew.

One could say there was an odd bond between the men that might be labeled friendship. There is a concept of honor among thieves, and this may be the best way to explain it. Never imagine them sharing a meal in kindness, or strolling the streets wondering about the day. But they did respect each other's skills and found they each grew in their accounts for the strengths of the other.

For twenty-five years, the two men grew more mean, more selfish, and more aligned in their purpose. The balance sheets changed over time for Scrooge and Marley, both that of the countinghouse and that of the character of each man, the one for the business going up and for the partners going down. Greed was ample in both men, but when the partnership began, Marley was certainly superior to Scrooge in applying it. As the years wore on, whether Scrooge learned or unleashed from within some greater ability to "out-Marley" Marley, there was at some point in time a moment, unmarked by any event, in which Scrooge became the master of the skill. His greed became more profound, more practiced, and more forged. Neither man could mark the transition, but they both knew when they had passed it. Once there, the firm's name became aptly worn.

4

Marley's health faded as he entered his seventieth year. The time had been filled with hatred when he should have been basking in the balm of love. No woman graced his life. No children called him Daddy or Grand-papa. He was willfully ignorant of whether he had nieces or nephews or whether his siblings still lived. No familial label of father, son, brother, or even friend was used in discussion of his name. Scrooge was his only true acquaintance, and as their bond was built not on mutual care but on mutual gain, it never rooted itself in the parts of the soul that, when touched, awaken men's senses to the truly beautiful and valuable in life.

He suffered with a cough that persisted through the fall

of that year. It was followed by chills and slow stiffening of his joints and muscles. He finally could not make it to his countinghouse, and on the twentieth of December, 1836, he was confined to his bedchamber, from which he would not again emerge in this life. Scrooge would call on him each morning and night, allegedly to see how he was and if he could provide anything for him. Yet there was coldness to the visits, as though Marley were approaching the end of his bodily lease and Scrooge were concerned he would not move out by the deadline.

On the morning of Christmas Eve, the end seemed near to the only people who even noticed Marley's approaching demise: the doctor, a nurse hired to spend these last few days at Marley's side, and Scrooge himself.

That morning, Scrooge had stopped by at his usual time in his usual foul manner, seeming especially disturbed that Marley had not completed his transition. The doctor was just finishing an examination as Scrooge walked into the room, the winter storm outside seeming to continue swirling around his cold character as he looked with impatient dissatisfaction upon the entire scene.

"Mr. Scrooge," the doctor said as he packed his stethoscope into his bag. "This will most likely be the day. He is unconscious most of the time, and when he has brief bits of clarity, he tries to speak, but it is senseless. I doubt he will make it to Christmas morning."

The doctor looked up from the tidying of his case to wait for a reaction from Scrooge. He was about to say what a shame it was to pass on this day, a time so celebrated with birth and hope, and thus to create a memory that would bring sadness with the thoughts of the season, but he held his tongue. He knew these men and their interests—or lack thereof—and on second thought surmised it was almost fitting that one of them should cross the bar at a time when the rest of the world celebrated.

Scrooge just stared at Marley, then took out his pocket watch and shook his head. The doctor shook his head as well as he watched this complete lack of compassion.

"Mr. Scrooge, there is really nothing to do. Given that, I will be with my son's family north of London over the holiday and will not be available. In addition, the nurse has asked that she take her leave of Mr. Marley, and I excused her this morning just before you arrived. It was an unnecessary expense when all she did was watch him sleep. There was no real comfort she could afford him."

Scrooge nodded, affirming the doctor's wise saving of Marley's money.

"Therefore, if Mr. Marley is going to have anyone with him, I suppose it will have to be you or someone else you arrange."

"I am a busy man, Doctor . . ."

"As am I, Mr. Scrooge. Where I can serve the sick and dying, I do so. Where there is nothing left to do but comfort, I leave that to family and friends." Looking back, he added, "And this one, I don't suppose anyone cares to comfort him, not even you, Mr. Scrooge. But that is none of my affair."

"You are correct. It is not. Good-bye, Doctor. I will let you show yourself out." The doctor left without another word.

"Humbug," Scrooge said to himself, and to Marley if he could possibly hear. In Scrooge's reckoning of life, in every inconvenience there needed to be a perpetrator. In this case, it was Jacob Marley for having the indecency to take his time with a protracted illness.

"Well, Jacob, I am busy. I am going to the counting-house to get some work done. I will return this afternoon. Should you choose to linger, well, that is your choice. I will take care of my business—you do the same with yours."

He had no idea if Marley had heard a word of it. He

donned his hat, wrapped his muffler about his neck, and strode out of the room, slamming the door with a final registration of his displeasure with Jacob Marley.

But Jacob had understood him. This had been one of those rare moments in which the fog of his mind had cleared. He was going to use the thin slice of opportunity to try to tell Ebenezer which accounts needed attending to that day, but the words would not come. So, struck dumb by his condition, he listened to Scrooge.

All of a sudden, Marley's mind had a flash of insight that was unparalleled in his life. He was astounded as he saw with his consciousness everything that had led to this moment. Every thought, every decision, every act of all his days worked together to force his life through a sluice that now contained all he was. A light shone somewhere in his understanding, illuminating a thought that startled him, an understanding unfamiliar but so clear he questioned if he had ever truly known anything before it. He had never really believed Scrooge was his friend, or even that such dysfunctional human contracts as friendship based on nothing but association were even necessary. He knew that Scrooge was a mean old scrape, knew it better than anyone other than Scrooge himself. What was new to Marley at this time was the simple understanding that Scrooge simply did not care.

It struck him that he perhaps could have endured more easily Scrooge's malice than his indifference. For in Scrooge's not caring, Jacob realized that, as far as he knew, nobody cared. Not one single soul on earth cared about him, thought of him, wished him well, or even wanted to say good-bye as he completed his life.

Was this not what he had asked for? Had he not told Melinda and his brothers to stay away? Had he not bitten every hand of friendship offered him? Was he not enjoying the solitude he had sought his entire adult life?

He was, and that was the bitter realization. For he was so competent, so driven, so independent that, in a temporal sense, he had never really needed anyone. This ability was now his curse, for he craved a friend in his final hours. His earthly assets, all of them, were down the street in the countinghouse, measured in ounces and pounds, and by morning, he would have lost his grasp on them. He did not even have a will, having been dissatisfied with simply giving his hard-earned estate to one who had not worked for it. He yearned for someone to tell him his life had been successful, to affirm that the single turn he had gotten upon earth had been well spent.

Scrooge was that one person who might have thus consoled him. But Jacob realized that he was no more than an entry in Scrooge's ledger—in an account that was now being closed.

Anger welled deep within him. Did Scrooge not realize what Jacob had done for him? Did he not understand what the opportunity to be partner had meant to his career? For all the value he accumulated over the almost thirty years they had worked together, did he not feel that it would warrant even one kind word to Marley!

What a wretched man, Marley thought. *Whatever in the world made him?*

Whether it was seconds or minutes, Marley did not know, but he paused so completely he thought his heart had stopped beating.

I did, were his own words that came to him. *I did. I made Ebenezer Scrooge.*

He then began to see apparitions. He knew they were not ghosts, but they haunted him nonetheless. They did not speak with him, but each of them looked at him. They were his clients. They looked not with hatred, not with fear, but with a sort of sorrow, as though it was not they who had lost at the hand of Marley's dealings, but Marley himself. One by one the faces went by. Those he had evicted from their homes. Those whose loans he had called in. Those who had stayed secure in their payments, but who knew as well as Marley that they had paid many times over the interest appropriate in the market for their type of loan. He saw faces from forty years prior and those from a week ago. He saw children in the cold, mothers with ragged shawls wrapped about them, fathers trying to care for the needs of their families against the frigid winds of Jacob Marley's contracts.

He struggled to speak, but he could only cry out in his mind, *What do you want of me? It was your doing, your choices that put you where you were. I lie here dying—I could do nothing for you even if I wanted to. Leave me be!*

But they kept coming. And though in life he had possessed little memory and no care for those he had hurt, somehow, in this spiritual interlude between life and death, he knew them all. He knew their situations and just what he had done.

"I had to do it—it was in our agreement!" he yelled at no one of them in particular.

Then it hit him. He had not needed to do it. He had chosen to do it. He had chosen to show no mercy, no caring. Business was his gospel, the contract his god, and he had been its zealous disciple, allowing no room for the spirit of the law but only for the letter.

And what had he gained for his strict adherence to the agreements so carefully conceived as to assure his success? He had gained a great deal of money. He had gained a reputation for intelligence and business savvy, and he had gained the freedom from relationships he had wished for. And all these gains were dispersing into the mist. They were his covering, his adornments, and when they vanished, there was nothing left but a sick, lonely old crust of a man.

Why had he not seen? What had prevented him from understanding? It was his selfishness that had driven him far from his spirit, and now that self-absorption had turned to allow him, in a final, cruel view of his life, to see just how far he had wandered, as he contemplated the enormity of his loss.

Somehow, during his insight, the entire day passed. As the clock struck a quarter past four, he heard the door open and someone enter. Feeling the cold waft in from the unheated house on his weakened limbs, he knew it would have to be Scrooge.

Scrooge looked briefly at Marley, uttered some epithet, and then put his valise on the table. He removed his winter coat and apparel and sat himself before his papers, beginning to work, as though Marley were nothing more than a fire in the hearth he was waiting to see go out.

Marley watched Scrooge. He had come to know the expressions of Ebenezer: the movement of his eyebrows that indicated he may have found a loophole in a potential agreement, the purse of his lips as he created a method to fill that hole to his advantage, and the set of his jaw as he crafted the language to assure his return. All these expressions were today present as Scrooge labored over his papers.

Marley thought about the day of their meeting. Scrooge had been a hardened nut as a young man, without a doubt. However, Marley knew that he had helped fashion the Scrooge he saw before him now. He had encouraged his greed. He had widened his purview of opportunity of the means of gain. He had shared in his spoils. He had worked ill with Scrooge, and offered no alternative.

Scrooge, he called out in his mind. *Look. Look at what we have done.* But no words left his lips, and there was therefore no final plea to reach Scrooge.

At one point, someone rapped the knocker

downstairs, and Scrooge left to answer the door. He returned with a man Marley did not recognize.

Scrooge and the man had begun to speak when the visitor noticed Marley on his bed. "Good heavens, man, he is right here!"

"Pay him no mind. He is long gone. He only hangs on in his body and will be done soon enough. He doesn't hear us."

"But he looks at us."

"He doesn't. He only looks this way. Besides, he will be dead before midnight."

Somewhat uncomfortably, the man turned back to their negotiations.

"Mr. Scrooge, are you quite sure Mr. Marley wanted this house transferred to your name? I would be much more comfortable if he were . . . more aware."

With diminishing patience, Scrooge said, "I am quite sure Mr. Marley wanted this. Why would he have let the deed to his property revert to the state when I was his only friend in the world?"

Scrooge clearly was not planning to allow the last minutes of Jacob's life to interfere with the transaction.

Marley's rage grew in his chest, soon giving way to horror. *Why did I not see this until now?* he thought.

I saw it, I knew, he chastised himself. *I set the example for Scrooge. I taught him his ways. I would be doing no differently today if our situations were reversed.*

Gently, but suddenly, mists began to swirl about Marley. At first, he felt an odd sense of peace. The mists were inviting, comforting, but firm in their purpose. He allowed himself to be cradled by their caresses.

Then he panicked. *This is it! I am done!*

The mists seemed to respond, almost saying to him, "Do not fear, this is the way."

No! Not yet. I need a moment, just one more!

The mists were not abusive in their grasp of him and were not unpleasant. But, despite this, they were no less determined. Marley tried to brace himself against their carriage as he leaned in toward Scrooge. Of course, his body was not moving, but his entire soul seemed to have a human form of its own. He positioned his spiritual legs to hold him back and tried to cry out to Scrooge. It was as in a dream when one strives to cry out but cannot find the voice. He pushed his mouth to open, his vocal cords to work, trying to connect his spirit with his body. And, just as in the dream when we finally have success, yelling out and waking ourselves from our slumber, Marley managed all of a sudden to call out from his temporal form, "Ebenezer . . ."

Scrooge looked up, frustrated at the second interruption to their negotiations brought on by the ailing Marley, but curious at the sound he had made. Scrooge stood and walked over to Marley's bedside. He did not crouch in caring attentiveness but stood surveying the sickened form, looking down at him from both his height and attitude.

"Ebenezer," Marley forced out again. He stared intently into Scrooge's eyes, trying to communicate the importance of his words. Scrooge turned an ear toward him, seeming to understand that he was trying to say something.

Marley took a breath, feeling the pain in his lungs and heart as he did so. His grip upon life continued to slip. He would not succumb until he got out these last words.

"I . . . am . . . sorry," he forced out.

Scrooge stared with obvious disgust.

"And . . . I forgive . . . you . . ." he exhaled.

Scrooge smirked. "Look at you, poor, poor Jacob. Do yourself the favor of not making a spectacle of your death. Honestly, man, this is degrading to us both. If you are going to die, get on with it."

Marley's eyes turned from Scrooge in sadness.

"What did he say?" the man with Scrooge gasped, staring in horror at the body that had emitted the last desperate sound.

Marley's final connection to this life was in watching Scrooge as he stared at the body on the bed and hearing him say, "I have no idea. Some final, incoherent, guttural death rattle, I suppose."

Marley's heart had stopped. His last breath passed. To Scrooge, he looked dead as a doornail. But Marley's still eyes took in one more scene, his ears one last sound.

Scrooge took a deep breath, turned, and said to his visitor, "Here, the day is waning, we need to conclude this arrangement and be done with it!"

The man shivered with the cold that seems to fill the void when the light of a life suddenly ends, and also with the chill that existed where Scrooge's soul should have been.

Marley's cry, rather than waking him from a dream, pushed him entirely into it. He fell backward into the arms of the mists, giving in to their comfort and passing from earthly life for good.

5

When Jacob came to, it was as if he had just emerged rejuvenated from the most peaceful slumber of his life. He felt no pain, no fear, no hunger, and no want of any kind. Though it had been just seconds since he lay in his bedchamber, he had already forgotten the torturous strains that had wracked his body. He was standing. He looked about and found himself in a warm mist. This was not dreary, cold, and dirty like the coal-smoke-laced fog of London. There was nothing sharp or abrasive in it. As he turned, he realized that his joints moved with fluidity. No lumbago crooked his back; no arthritis stiffened his hands. He clenched and unclenched his fists, feeling the flexibility in his fingers and marveling at the smoothness of his skin. He ran his hands across his cheeks and fore-head, finding the wrinkles of his many years gone. Grabbing his ponytail, he pulled it into view, seeing with pleasure the dark tones that had graced it in his youth.

He also felt something familiar. It was an old feeling, from long ago. It was pleasant—no, more than pleasant: it was joyful. The feeling was both in him and about him. He looked about to identify it, but there was nothing to focus on. He could tell he was seeing, but there seemed to be nothing to see. Then, slowly appearing, there was a person, if you could call him that, standing in front of him.

He was clearly a man, but so perfectly formed, the word seemed almost an insult in its description. He stood erect and stared intently at Marley. He was not young, but not old. His build and skin might peg him in his twenties, but he wore a visage of wisdom that one might see in an ancient fellow. Of all his features, so pristine was the beauty of his face, Marley could not take his eyes off him. There was a composure, a balance, a completeness to his countenance that was perfection to Marley. As he wondered at it all, the man seemed to speak to him without moving his lips.

"Jacob, what you see is peace."

Marley just stared, caught unawares by the sudden communication of such perfect clarity. Rather than its coming to his ears, he heard it in his mind and soul.

Finally, meekly, and with trepidation, Marley stammered a question, "Are you . . . Him?"

The man smiled kindly. "No, Jacob, I am not. I am one of very many who assist in His work. That is all."

"This feeling I feel from you, Spirit, it is one so unusual to me and yet there is a familiarity to it at the same time. Like a smell from a good meal long ago, bringing back all the feelings of that moment. I recall it, but I cannot name it."

"Do you wish to know what it is, Jacob?"

"I do, Spirit." He paused. "Or, I think I do. I fear, in a way I cannot explain, that the understanding of this feeling will both edify me and somehow condemn me."

"Oh, Jacob," the spirit said with a wise smile, "this feeling could never condemn. It is the most basic, the most fundamental element of life—not just the life you left, and not just this one, but all life, of all things in all times. It is the marrow of our existence."

"Tell me, then. I know of nothing that could be so comprehensive."

"You actually do, Jacob. You may not have known its

breadth and depth in your adult years, but you knew its ways as a youth. It is very simple, and its simplicity is part of its beauty. This, Jacob, is love."

Jacob was speechless. He looked down, though there seemed to be nothing to look at. He started to pace back and forth, though he knew not what surface supported him, nor what he was suspended over or held beneath.

"Love," he muttered under his breath. "Love." Looking at the kindly, perfect man, he said, "Spirit, this love: I felt it as a boy, as you said, and I suppose that it is what I am recalling. But in my recent years, or I should say—and I am sure you know—in all my years since then, I have been a stranger to love. As I saw it approaching me in life, I stepped to the other side of the road until it passed, and eventually it ceased to look for me and I ran into it no more. I dare say I should know nothing of it. And yet," he almost laughed, "I sit here now and I feel I know all about it. How can this be?"

"Because, Jacob, you are completely surrounded by love—unconditional, everlasting love."

Jacob looked steadily at the man. His years of negotiating had trained him to search the face for some insight about what a person was saying. Did he flinch in a way that revealed he was lying? Did he choose his words with such care as to construct a detour around an important fact? Did he answer too quickly, indicating his anxiety over some point, or too slowly, showing his discomfort? Jacob found nothing in the peaceful visage. Only, as the spirit had stated, love.

Jacob spoke more directly. "Spirit, I am not an ignorant man. I know how I have lived my life. In fact, just minutes ago, it all became clear to me."

This pained Jacob to say, but he pressed on through the discomfort. "I have not loved others. Love? I have not even cared for others. Why, people's lives have been a bother to me. This love, comforting though it may be, I am afraid will be my prosecutor. How could it not be so?"

"Jacob, love does not prosecute. It seeks neither revenge nor dominance. It does not win at the cost of someone else's loss. Love only accepts, completely and without reservation."

"But, Spirit, my mistakes . . . I don't have the words. On my deathbed that last day—today, or yesterday, whenever it was—I saw parade in front of me the faces of those I had ignored or hurt. I don't know why I could look upon them in life and yet be blind to them at the same time, but I was just so blind."

Jacob began to cry as the weight of his actions

became clearer to him. "Love must have its limit! It cannot possibly cover all I have done." He looked up to the spirit, vulnerability etching his features.

The spirit had compassion in his eyes as he said, "Love's purpose is not to hide our errors. Love's purpose is to forgive them. That is very different."

Jacob was shocked. "Are you telling me that none of the wrong I committed in my life mattered? In the end, myself and the man I threw out on the street, we will be peers in this place? He is entitled to no more than I? Though I cannot imagine what could be more than this—this heaven, or whatever it is."

The spirit looked deeply at Jacob, who swore he saw tears in his eyes. "Jacob, what will prosecute you is not love, but yourself."

"How so, Spirit?"

"The clarity of truth will illuminate your soul with understanding, as it has already started to do, but that understanding will be a burden as well. Remorse and regret will increase with that understanding, and you may shrink from its weight, pulling yourself far from this peace."

The spirit continued, "And Jacob, you are not a peer with Jonathan."

"Who?"

"Jonathan, Martin, Ezra, Peter. And their wives, their children—just a few of the many for whom you made life more difficult. We know them all by name. Jacob, you had many opportunities to serve man, you know that. But you did not turn those opportunities into any act of kindness. So, no, you are not peers. However, you did something very unusual. In that last day on earth, you opened your eyes for the first time in a long time—in fact, for the first time since you dropped your connection to your grandfather Thelonius."

"You know about that?"

"We know about all your life, Jacob. We know about Thelonius. We know why your father gave you his name. We know what he hoped for in his heart as you were christened in St. George's church, cradled in his loving arms. In his every hug of your small frame, we felt his caring for you."

The spirit then looked sorrowful. "We know the pain he felt as you discarded that name from your life. We watched him pray for you, reach out to you, offering so many calls to come back, all ignored. We watched him die, your name, your full name, the last words on his lips."

Jacob was silent. The scenes of his father loving him passed before him in his understanding. His heart ached.

"Spirit," he uttered softly, "why did someone not tell me? Did not anyone care enough to warn me what I was becoming?"

"Jacob," he said imploringly, "every day of your life we called to you."

"I never heard you!"

"We reached out to you in every way possible. In thoughts and feelings, by the interactions of others in your way. Why, even your name—that was a sign for you to remember your heritage, to feel the possibility of greatness that was in you. But you discarded it."

"Spirit, I didn't know. I . . ."

The spirit was firm. "Jacob, you did know! Ask yourself. Did you really not know?" Then the spirit smiled and spoke more softly. "When you stood in school on the first day and the master asked all of you your names, you did not say your own but in fact proclaimed it! You said it with testimony. 'Jacob Thelonius Marley, sir.' Do you remember?"

"I do," Jacob said, replaying that memory in his mind. "I felt I was something special because of that name."

"You were, Jacob, you were! You were bound for marvelous things. That name was more than a means to call you. It was a crest, a shield, and an Excalibur, all in one."

"But I set it aside."

"You did. But we did not give up on you, Jacob. Man makes mistakes. It does not change our love for him."

"Then, Spirit, tell me why I am here and not . . ." he motioned downward with his head, "there."

"You finally saw, and with that vision, you did something of infinite worth. You apologized. And you forgave. These are two of the greatest gifts one man can give another."

Jacob responded with emotion. "But I could not speak clearly. Ebenezer knows not of my sorrow for what I have done. And these others, Spirit," he said as he hung his head, "I don't even know their names."

"True, Jacob." The spirit seemed to cradle him with his eyes, full of the love he had spoken of, but also full of sorrow and pain in Jacob's behalf. "And this is a great duty left undone. Many have had to struggle with the hate they felt for you over what you did to them. But that is their burden to resolve. Jacob, you did acknowledge your errors, and that is in your favor. You have a great deal to learn in this existence, but at least you have come pointed in the right direction."

Jacob felt no comfort. "But I cannot withstand it. Spirit, the voices cry out to me. I hear now what I would not hear for years. The pain of not caring burns me like a brand. What can I do?"

"You can learn . . ."

"But what can I do for *them?*" he emphasized. "How can I replace what I have taken?"

"They must find their own way now. You have finished that chapter of your life."

Marley was anxious. He paced and wrung his hands. All the pain of a life wasted seemed to be bearing down on him, crowding out the love he had felt up until now. But in all of his emotions, all the disharmony that was agitating his soul, there was one thought more overpowering than the rest.

"Spirit, I know you must have a plan for men like me, and I do not mean to disparage your comments. But there is something I have done that I cannot survive the torment of without resolution. All the ill I have rendered, I have multiplied many times over through one set of acts. Spirit, it is what I have done to Ebenezer."

He looked up, but the spirit said nothing. He just held his gaze, listening with complete attention.

"Spirit, at every turn, I have led him astray. I have taught him my ways, which I know are not yours. I have supported him in his greed. I have condoned his actions. I took not one opportunity, *not one*, to try to offer a bit of advice that might have lifted his or another's heart. He yet lives, and my legacy of greed lives with him and, I fear, will condemn him in the end."

Jacob looked up with tears in his eyes. "Spirit, if you stand for good in all men, if you seek to have me learn, if this love you speak of has any mercy in it, you must let me do something to try to help Ebenezer. As you say, my time is done, but he yet carries out my directions and business, continuing to damage the lives of others as though I lived on. For the sake of my own death, please let me stop the momentum I have created!" Jacob sobbed, "Oh, Spirit, I pray thee, let me do something!"

The spirit looked at him thoughtfully for a minute, appearing to study him. He then said, "Jacob Thelonius Marley, I will tell you what you can do, but once you hear and understand it, I do not know that you will want to take that path."

After a pause in which he seemed to try to impress Jacob with the weight of what was coming, he said: "The fate of souls varies according to the workings of their life. A great deal of good is rendered by most people, but they are no strangers to error, either. There is the possibility, for some, to have yet another chance, in another way, to leave good in some small fashion in the path of those they wish to help. In the process, they grow as well."

"Well, Spirit, that sounds perfect!" Jacob said hopefully. "In this capacity I can serve Scrooge."

"The difficulty is that you are not like most people, Jacob," the spirit said as he put an arm about his shoulder. "We love you so, and we feel the pain you feel. Remorse is an unrelenting taskmaster. When one has lived as you did most of your life, choosing at every prompting to take rather than give; to avoid rather than proclaim truth; to turn his back coldly to need, asserting that the beggars have brought their suffering upon themselves, rather than show mercy; then that person's fate is different." He stopped, almost as though he did not want to continue.

"Spirit, what is it? Hold nothing back from me."

"Jacob, such a spirit is consigned to wander the earth. To visit every station in which he was presented with an opportunity to do good but did not. To see what became of those who were placed in his path so that he could lighten their burdens, but who rather suffered from his lack of compassion. To feel the pain of unresolvable regret—this, Jacob, is hell. It is far worse than any fire and brimstone man has conjured."

"How long must these spirits wander?"

"Always."

"But after they have visited these places?"

"Then they go again. For you see, Jacob, life moves on and the impact of their decisions continues to unfold. Sometimes the pain is in seeing what good they might have done, only to see another do it. Sometimes, however, they see those instances in which it was theirs alone to succor their brother or sister. Having missed that chance by choice, they watch the cascade of human events that comes as a result, sometimes affecting generations. This, Jacob, is unbearable, but must be borne."

"And . . . is this my fate?"

"No. As I said, Jacob, you did a marvelous thing in your final moments. You forgave, and this is, as it is said on your world, divine."

Jacob was incredulous. "And for this one act, I am freed from wandering?"

"Yes, you are. These are powerful strokes. It is not their numbers or duration that weighs in the balance, but their sincerity and intent."

The spirit was serious in his next statement: "But, Jacob, you have only begun to understand; you have at best only rudimentary insights. You have a great deal to learn, and that will be painful as well in this world. You will be no stranger to regret in this condition, as you can already tell. But you are not prepared, not experienced enough to go help Ebenezer."

Jacob pondered this condition. "Spirit, may I make a proposal?"

"A proposal? Jacob, this is not a negotiation."

"An idea, then. A thought. May I share it?"

"Go ahead," the spirit invited.

"I know what you say is true. I know nothing of the heart of man, and I stand in no position to try to teach another. But, Spirit, the experiences of my life may qualify me to do one thing. I know the plane upon which Scrooge lives, for so I lived myself. If he cannot hear the whispers of spirits, if he cannot heed their warnings, if he cannot or will not see their light, perhaps I might hold a lesser light, one he will see. If I can do nothing but suggest to him there is another way, then perhaps those who show him that way may find someone who is open to their guidance."

The spirit continued to watch Jacob patiently, the slightest sense of approval in his gaze.

"Spirit, you said there are others who sought my welfare. There must be those of your world still willing to do the same for Scrooge. Would they take this opportunity to try to turn him if I opened a crack in his shell?"

"Perhaps, but these others must be convinced both of your sincerity and of your ability to do so."

"I must recruit them, then?"

"You must convince them. But Jacob, their hands will not be forced. There are many here who have tried to reach Ebenezer, but he is deaf and blind to their efforts."

"Spirit, I can do it. I know the man. I wish I did not, for that knowledge is no testament to any goodness in me. In many ways, he is the mirror of me. In other ways," Jacob sighed, "far worse. But I think I know the language of what is left of his soul. I can get him to hear."

The spirit was silent. Jacob felt him surveying all his thoughts and intents. The pause was long, but Jacob would not interrupt it.

Finally, the spirit said, "Jacob, you may try. But there is much to be done."

Jacob leaned forward with anxiety. "Let me be about it quickly, then!"

"First, you must convince the spirits who may assist you to help. It is their decision—not mine, and not yours. If they say no, they have their reasons and there is no argument."

"Agreed," Jacob said quickly.

"Then, though you feel remorse, you know very little of the damage done by your life. If you choose this path, you must be consigned to the dreary wanderings we spoke of, and you must confront the echoes of your life. This is part of your choosing, and you may not pick among its conditions. It will not be pleasant, and you may even forget about Ebenezer as you are consumed by the sorrow you will feel. But this experience is necessary if you are to help him."

Less enthusiastically, but with equal resolve, Jacob said, "I understand."

"Finally, you must then be successful in helping Ebenezer listen. His time on earth is not much longer. If you do not reach him prior to the moment that is marked for his demise, then he will be lost to the same fate you are entering into."

"And me, Spirit, what of me then?"

"Your desires are valiant. Regardless of Ebenezer's reaction to your efforts, you will come back here and begin your progression. Though I warn you, if Scrooge is not reclaimed, your own realization of that failure will be heavy to bear."

"Spirit, then let me select this road. I beg of you,

allow me the opportunity to reach him and undo what burdens I have laid upon this man."

The spirit nodded his assent.

Marley then asked, "Spirit, can you tell me, how much time does he have?"

"His body is old, but worse, his heart is hard. There is no affection that eases his years. He has not long—that is all I will say."

"Spirit, when do I find others to help?"

"Now, Jacob. You will have a moment with them. You cannot meet these spirits. When Scrooge is ready, and you are ready, when this confluence occurs, they will show themselves to you. Now, you can only put your petition out to them. You may speak, but they will not answer. They see you, but not you them. You can only make your appeal to them, and they will decide."

"How will I know their answer?"

"You will know when it is right."

Jacob looked about, not knowing which way to turn to address those who might be listening. As he saw no one, the nature of the situation caused him to feel that if he looked up, he might be working in the right general direction.

"Spirits," he said with a trembling voice, "whoever

you are, and wherever you are, I am Jacob . . ." he paused and then, with care, uttered a word he had not said in a long time, " . . . Thelonius . . . Marley."

His kindly companion, who had seated himself upon something unseen to Jacob, leaned forward and said, "That part is not necessary. They know who you are."

"Yes, of course," Jacob whispered.

"And they can hear you. A whisper is not concealing anything."

Jacob nodded in understanding. "What do they know of me?"

"Everything. I am afraid that does not help your cause."

Returning to his upward gaze, Jacob said, "Spirits, I have . . . I have . . ."

Jacob looked down and shook his head. He could see none of them, but somehow, he could tell they were patient in waiting for him to find the words. After many moments, he raised his gaze high again and said, "Spirits, I have betrayed mankind. I have betrayed my family, my associates, and my friends. Well, I suppose I don't have friends. I rejected that affiliation. I have cultivated greed wherever I have gone. I have sought only gain for myself.

I cannot count the men I have wounded, but one in particular, Ebenezer Scrooge of London—"

The spirit interrupted. "They know him, too. Quite well. That also does not help."

"To Ebenezer, then, I have served as a poor example. I know we are all our own men, but I did every possible thing to ward off any opportunity he may have had of changing his heart. Whatever you have done for him in his life, I feel I have undone. Spirits, I pray thee, grant me an opportunity to assist in reclaiming this man. I go to wander. I know not when I shall see you, or if I will see you at all. But, Spirits, I beg for your help. I must undo the damage I alone have done. I will try to reach him, and if I do, I beg you, would you then try one more time in his behalf, for his sake, to help him?"

Quiet settled again upon the scene. There was no response expected, and none came. Jacob's last words reverberated in his mind, the question hanging in space, waiting to be taken up by the spirits whom he had petitioned.

The grand man of peace who had greeted Jacob approached him and put his hand upon his shoulder. Softly, he said, "That was well done. You could do no more. If there is a way, that will have done it. If not, nobody could have done better."

"But will it be good enough?"

"I know not. Time will tell. But your appeal was heard, I can assure you."

"Can you see them?"

"Them, and many more, Jacob."

"Could you see their faces?"

"I can see their hearts," the spirit said.

"Can you tell me anything, Spirit? Before I depart to confront my life, is there any comfort you can give me that there is perhaps a chance they may be prevailed upon to help? Spirit, is there any shred of hope?"

"They are considering, Jacob, but that is mostly yet to be decided. Now, you must go. This path you are to follow is not easy. I wish you well. Remember, you have chosen this. Farewell, Jacob."

"Farewell. And, Spirit . . ."

"Yes?"

"Thank you."

6

The first thing Marley was aware of was the nearly instantaneous loss of the peace he had enjoyed when in the presence of the kindly spirit. Though he had felt his own remorse while with the spirit, he had been buoyed up somehow. Now, as that support withdrew, he wondered how he had ever withstood the pain of his actions.

This, however, was not his final state. He felt a great, crushing weight upon him. It was unlike anything he had experienced, pressing in upon his entire self from every direction. His arms were heavy, his legs were heavy, and his heart was heavy. As he tried to move, he felt as if he were pulling his limbs through a thick coagulation more of mud than of air. He looked down to see what restrained him, and as he gazed at his arms, he began to see chains. They were not burnished bright, like new metal, or covered with rust, like old. They were formed as chains, but they were of some other matter, almost seeming to be extensions of his body. He was bound in them; they wrapped themselves about his arms, then his torso, then over his shoulders. As he tried to move, they became heavier. They held in their links the emblems of his life: not gifts, not people, not pleasant memories, but contracts and cash boxes and locks and keys. These were the only things that had mattered to him. In life, his greatest pleasure had been to feel the heft of the metal box filled with rewards of his work. That heft now burdened him. Each ounce of gain that had at one time brought him pleasure was now a pound of pain. He looked at the box closest to him. He knew that latch, those hinges, and the feel of the key in the lock. Yet it was as ghostly as himself. He did not know man, but he knew his cash box. In it alone he had invested his life. And now, it alone would be his eternal companion.

He felt he could barely move, but move he must. He seemed to have no choice in the matter. He was not being forced by any outward power. The momentum of his living demanded his forward trudge in his death. He had no choice because he had chosen to leave himself no choice.

He heaved the weight up and took a step. The chains clanked and pulled. They chafed his apparitions of limbs as though his skin still encased him. It was beyond his strength to pull and beyond his will not to. A second step with equal drive. Step by step, Jacob walked into the present and future of those who suffered because of his past.

Each stride moved him forward, from inches at times to great distances at others, passing over the entire continent in one step. Yet there was no pleasure in his journey—no wind whipping about his head or thrill of rising above human limitations. Rather, each step was slow and painful, regardless of how far it took him. With each step, he could do no more. And, with each step, he must.

He knew not where to go, only to move forward and find himself in some new place. Some of these he knew, and in them, his cursing was to remember each life he had touched there, to see the impact of what he had done or left undone, and to have no recourse. There was no relief in the visit, no comfort from the confrontation. Rather, it only burned into his memory more brightly his sin toward man.

Then, at other times, there were places unfamiliar—places he should have visited through some set of circumstances that he had ignored or resisted. Though he had not been at that place in life, he was made aware of what his role could have been. He could see where he might have intervened, where he might have entered the stage of someone else's life but did not. Each visit was another death. The accumulated burden of the experiences was crushing, and it was growing all the time.

It would have been relief to suffer a final fate, to be banished from all existence, to cease to be in any form, but that oblivion would not come. There was no release.

Multiple times, he found himself in the counting-house, on the street, or in the Exchange, each time in the presence of Scrooge. When this first occurred, his heart—or what transparent remnant there was of it—leapt at the thought that perhaps the spirits had conceded to him and the time had arrived. He tried to call to Scrooge, but the old miser was unaware of Jacob's presence. He stood in his path, but Scrooge walked right through him, entirely ignorant. Jacob yelled, he scolded, he chastised, but all this dissipated into the silence that surrounded Scrooge. Finally, he understood this would be the way. It was not the condescension of the spirits, but more of his penance. He stood silently by, writhing in pain to see his character alive in Scrooge, who exercised his will upon others without compassion. Even knowing the boundary that separated them, still, countless times he begged Scrooge to stop, but Scrooge was deaf and blind to his presence.

When some unheard strike of an unseen clock occurred, he would be compelled to move off again to visit another place.

He saw countless others like him in his wanderings. They passed within a breath of each other, had there been breath to fill the gap. Yet there was never acknowledgment. Not one soul ever paid his respects to his fellow prisoner. Jacob supposed they saw him, as he did them, but there was no means to communicate. He could form thoughts in the words he had used all his life; he could even utter them in such a manner that he would hear, but no one else would. These souls were eternally disconnected, forever separated with a force that would not allow any interchange. They were like another race with no societal tie to each other, bound on their own miserable, independent journeys, alike only in the obvious countenance of pain. In this, therefore, was all final comfort dashed. They were not only alone but completely aware that they could only be alone. There would be no relationships, no words of courtesy, not even a bark of sympathetic discontent just to offer witness of each other's existence.

There was only one sound he could hear from outside his realm. It was common among all these lost souls, and yet each had its unique signature. It was a mournful wailing from the deepest reaches of pain in the heart. Each man and woman seemed not so much to emit the sound as to have it be the natural extension of their sorrow. They could not repress it, and it flew from them into the ether for all of their kind to hear, and none to console.

Marley lost most of his sense of time. He could not count hours or days, weeks or months. His only dark sundial of this dark sphere was in his visits to Scrooge, marking an annual passing. For, each time he found himself with Scrooge, he was surrounded by the wreaths and holly and food and general well-wishings of Christmas. Not that old Scrooge seemed to notice such things, other than to offer a scowl in their direction. But Jacob came to learn that it would be his lot, during the season known for softening men's hearts, to spend that season with the hardest heart of all. He saw Scrooge growing older, and, in that aging, watched the crust continue to form on him, insulating Ebenezer from any possible love in the world that might have resuscitated his ailing conscience.

When one waits up all night to see a sunrise, in the last moments, it seems it will never come, even though one knows the inevitability of it. If we find we lack faith in ourselves or in others, we can at least have faith in the trustworthiness of nature, that at the appointed time, the horizon will lighten in grand prelude to the sun throwing its morning shafts into our lives. But in Marley's case, other than his visits with Scrooge, he would experience one interminable night. When the hope of dawn felt inevitable, it would not come.

It was because of this that Jacob was startled when, for the first time since he had bade farewell to the spirit years ago, he heard a voice address him in his mind.

"Jacob."

"Yes, what, yes! Who is that?"

"It is I."

"But who are you?"

"I am one who heard your plea. The time has come. You are as ready as you can be. Scrooge is as ready as he can be. That may not be enough, but it is the time to try."

Jacob could scarcely believe it.

"I cannot see you, Spirit," Jacob said anxiously as he turned his form back and forth. "Where should I look?"

"You will see me in time, when Scrooge does, if Scrooge does."

"Do I know you?"

"No, you would not know me, though you might have in your life, had you looked. I tried to reach you many times, but you were dull to it."

"When, Spirit, when did I have that chance?"

"You will see. I know you well, Jacob—we all do."

"We?" he asked.

"Yes. There will be three of us. We will try to reach Scrooge, as you have pleaded. You have felt the pain of remorse, have you not?"

"Oh, Spirit," Jacob said with a sigh. "There truly can be no greater pain than this."

"Remorse is a heavy burden, but in its weight, it has great power to awaken men's souls. There are three realizations mankind can experience that might give them cause for change. First, remorse for what is gone but might have been in the past. Second, a shocking awareness of where they are in the present. Finally, fear for what will be in the future, should their paths not change. These three missions make up our cause."

"Spirit, since I don't know your name, which of these is your endeavor?"

"It matters not, Jacob. You must warn Ebenezer we are coming."

"But, Spirit, these years I have tried to reach him. My voice fails to penetrate his world. I don't know what to do."

"Jacob, your part is now to go be with Scrooge. If you are diligent, it will come to you. Go now. Ebenezer is in his countinghouse."

And with that, Jacob was there.

Marley's assistant, Duffin, was long gone, having been fired by Scrooge the morning after Marley's funeral for his exorbitant expense, which was not so much as an average wage. But in Scrooge's mind, if it could be gotten for less, it was better. In his place was a man diminutive in form and presence. Bob Cratchit had been hired by Scrooge for the primary asset of being cheap. Yet there was a goodness about his countenance—a purity Jacob could see, and a childlike innocence. Jacob saw Bob attempting to warm himself by a single coal.

"He cannot gain any warmth from that," Marley thought.

He leapt as he felt the spirit's voice.

"He cannot. But Ebenezer will give him no more fuel than that."

"Spirit, will we always communicate like this, you speaking to my mind? Will you be ever present with me from now on?"

"As I am needed, I will be there."

Turning back to Cratchit, Jacob said, "He would do best just to sit at his desk and work. The work of his hands would keep him warmer than his attempts to heat by that faint flame."

"Bob is a pure-hearted man, Jacob. He may not have the worldly intelligence so prized by men of your profession, but he has a heart that produces far more wisdom. He would have benefited by Scrooge's learning. And Ebenezer would have benefited from his perspectives.

They would have magnified each other and been a good pair."

Within the office, Marley and Scrooge's two old desks, which had sat facing each other, were gone. Scrooge had sold them both, purchasing a larger, more prestigious desk for himself, and it was at this grand edifice that he sat studying his ledgers. Jacob walked in, dragging his chains to a chair, and sat facing Scrooge. The chains made a scraping sound across the floor, a constant cacophony of links banging against the ironmongery of his trade. To Scrooge, of course, there was no apparition of Jacob, no sound, and not so much as a fleck of dust on the floor was moved in the wake of the dragging chains.

"What will allow me to reach you, old Scrooge?" Jacob wondered aloud.

With that, he was startled as a young man strode into the office.

"A merry Christmas, Uncle. God save you!"

Jacob was surprised. "Scrooge has a nephew, Spirit?"

"He does," the spirit offered. "A fine man, one of the best."

Jacob was amazed at the interaction between the two. Scrooge's nephew invited Scrooge to Christmas dinner. Scrooge declined, of course, as Christmas had always been a workday like any other for Jacob and Ebenezer. Yet the nephew persisted, and persisted and persisted again. Scrooge's rancor grew; he criticized the invitation, the holiday, and the nephew himself, eventually unleashing his full contempt in his cantankerous, disgust-riddled assessment of the man, the day, and its blessings.

"If I could work my will, every idiot who goes about with 'Merry Christmas' on his lips, should be boiled with his own pudding, and buried with a stake of holly through his heart. He should!"

In some extraordinary feat of self-control, the nephew did not match angry strokes with his uncle. Rather, the more he was pushed downward by Scrooge, the more his joy seemed to flow out of him. It was like the light of a lantern assaulting the early evening dusk, when the increasing darkness only seems to strengthen its beam. Marley was sure that at any moment, some repressed frustration would spring forth from the young man, battering old Scrooge with just what he wanted, the Christmas bubble popped in his face. But, not only did it not spring forth, it did not seem to exist. No man could repress it if it were there. The young relative of Scrooge seemed to be master of himself not by controlling his anger but by having none of it at all. He left as cheerful as he had entered.

Marley spent the afternoon in the old counting-house, an unseen companion to its two employees. Men called upon Scrooge looking for donations for the poor, and if one could never imagine he would treat anyone worse than his nephew, then they had only to watch how Scrooge dispensed with the agents of the destitute. He could not have done them as much damage by kicking them literally through the door as by what he said as he hastened them out. To the complete amazement of Bob Cratchit, Scrooge, and Marley too, they asked what level of donation Scrooge wished to make to the support of the less fortunate.

"I wish to be left alone," said Scrooge. "Since you ask me what I wish, gentlemen, that is my answer. I don't make merry myself at Christmas and I can't afford to make idle people merry. I help to support the establishments I have mentioned—they cost enough; and those who are badly off must go there."

"Many can't go there; and many would rather die," the men offered, still imagining they were giving some useful information desired by the old man.

"If they would rather die," said Scrooge, "they had better do it, and decrease the surplus population."

Jacob said nothing to the spirit, but the spirit, sensing his feelings, spoke to him. "It is painful to the soul to watch, isn't it?"

"Those are my words, Spirit," Jacob said quietly. "I said them about the death of Scrooge's sister."

"Well, never wonder if you were a strong influence on the man."

Jacob stared silently at the room, which seemed somehow devalued by the departure of the two solicitors. Eventually, he spoke again to the spirit. "Spirit, could those men sense Scrooge's contempt?"

"Yes, they could."

"Then why did they continue? Why did they not run from him?"

"They are driven by an inner voice. They felt right in being here. They thought Scrooge might relent."

Marley almost laughed. "It seems to me their consciences would have better steered them to any other businessman on this street—indeed, to any other businessman in London—to get their contribution."

"Perhaps," the spirit offered, "the contribution they sought was not as important as the one they had to give."

"Give? What did they give other than to throw fuel upon a fire?"

"Jacob, this was a chance. Had Ebenezer just listened for a moment, had he let one ice crystal on that frozen heart thaw enough, he might have given just a shilling to get them out, and in so doing experienced a speck of the joy of giving, which might have led to something more."

"Unlikely," said Jacob.

"Yes. That is why we help, because it is unlikely otherwise. These chances are all about trying to help him. Like this one."

"What one?"

"Listen . . ."

Marley heard a faint, young voice begin to sing outside the door of the countinghouse.

> *God rest you merry, gentlemen,*
> *Let nothing you dismay.*

With that, Scrooge was off in a huff to chase the owner of the pure tones away.

"He tried," Marley heard the spirit say.

"That caroler, he was prompted too?"

"He was," the spirit said.

"Are spirits so involved in men's lives?" Marley asked.

"Mankind is involved in men's lives. We only help them know how."

The singer went his way, and the voice of the spirit continued, "Jacob, all around you, every day, as you walk the miles of earth, there are calls to your spirit and to all others' spirits as well. They come from your fellow beings and from life itself: the way the sun highlights a tree, a bird song lilting across the morning, the smell of flowers. All these are for your joy, but also for more. They call you."

Scrooge dismissed his clerk with an especially sour flair, donned his coat and hat, and headed for the door.

Jacob watched Scrooge leave the warehouse and hurried to pursue him as best he could with the weight he bore. He followed him to a tavern, where Scrooge took his dinner. Scrooge sat there engrossed in some thought as he stared first into the evening papers and then into a ledger he had taken with him. Marley thought of what the spirit had said. He closed his eyes and listened. He heard the ever-present mourning of those about him, traversing in their chains the walks of life. Marley did his best to block them out.

"What, Spirit? What can I do? I will do it if you would but show me."

The spirit said nothing, but all of a sudden something occurred to Marley. *Home.* That was it. He needed to go to Scrooge's home, his old home.

Being satisfied with that conclusion, he opened his eyes and found himself standing upon the step of that same house, looking into the street.

He did not move. He did not know why he was here, but he was not about to move until he found his purpose in standing sentinel at the door of the old building.

In time, he saw Ebenezer coming along, looking down to watch his step and fiddling for his key. Marley looked at him and muttered under his breath, "Spirit, help me reach him."

As if on cue, Scrooge inserted the key and looked up, precisely into the eyes of Jacob. As Jacob had suffered his sentence these many years, he had come to disregard the physical borders of human life. Walls served only to help him recognize a place, rather than to limit where he could go. He realized then that he stood precisely on the threshold, and in so doing he was standing in the same place as the closed door.

As Scrooge looked at him, for the first time since

his death, Marley saw Scrooge see him. For in the place where the brass door-knocker hung was Marley's face, melded into its form—still brass, but distinctly Marley. Scrooge looked into Marley's eyes, first with a brief bit of surprise, then with curiosity, then skepticism, all in a moment. Marley stared back, unmoving, afraid to alter whatever combination of universal elements had somehow allowed this event. He knew not what to do, so he continued to gaze at Ebenezer.

After several moments of their seeing one another, Scrooge muttered some epithet under his breath, looked down, and unlocked the door, dismissing the experience. He proceeded to walk right though Marley without even knowing it.

Marley turned and watched as Scrooge began to ascend the wide, palatial stairs, which stood as an artifact, silently testifying as to their once-grand purpose.

All of a sudden he started as he saw shadows pass around and through him up the stairs. Scrooge, who was ahead of him, stopped and appeared to notice something as well.

"Spirit," said Marley, "is that . . . a hearse?"

"It is."

"Why does a hearse ascend his stairs?"

"It is a premonition for Scrooge. A foreshadowing and a warning."

"Warning of what?"

"You were told his time is short. Now that time is near the end. Think of yourself, Jacob. Why is it that on your deathbed, you considered for the first time the wrongness of the path you had trod? Why, in that one day, did you have more insight, and in turn act on that insight, than in all your other days of earthly existence?"

Jacob closed his eyes, remembering what he had remembered thousands of times during his travels. "It was the reality of it. We all know death comes, but it is so distant to our present condition it is not real. When you confront it in a way that affirms you have arrived at that fearful station, all your senses change."

"That is right," the spirit affirmed. "Your world often mourns the 'unlucky soul' who suffers a long illness. But this is a gift! It allows the sufferer just this kind of experience. But many, for various reasons, are taken in a heartbeat—or, in Scrooge's case, that lack of one."

"His heart will stop?"

"At this time, I see it will. It is only kindness on the spirits' parts that such a strange vision as a hearse might awaken that sullen soul to the coming reality of his death, and thereby afford him the benefit you had of the confrontation of its reality."

Jacob seemed alarmed. "Spirit, how near is this end? Is it measured in your time?"

"His time."

"How long does he have, then?"

"His hour is tonight, before the dawn of Christmas. Scrooge has been influenced over the years by as many opportunities as any man, given all the chances anyone could have. If you can convince him to believe in what he sees this night, and if his visit into the shadows of his past causes him to see his own wrongdoing, then he will be given an additional night to confront the conditions and effects of how he lives in the present. If he can reach beyond his blind eyes to see what impact he has upon others, if there is one shred of learning, he will then be given yet another gift of one more night to contemplate his future. If his understanding of what will come in that future alters his path, he will tarry longer on this earth, and his time stretches out beyond my sight."

"But, Spirit, if his past does not move him, then he dies?" Jacob asked.

"Yes, then he dies tonight."

"Spirit, why did you wait until now? Did I wander all

this time so that there could be only moments left to possibly influence his heart?"

"It was not my choice, Jacob. It was Ebenezer's. Not a day has passed that some effort to redeem him has not been undertaken, even while you wandered. Do not think we have waited idly by these past years. This is the night because it is the time in which he may be influenced."

Jacob stared at the disappearing image of Scrooge. Moments later, he heard his bedroom door close and the locks thrown.

"The image of the hearse did not affect him," Jacob observed.

"No, it did not. He saw it. He dismissed it." Then the spirit's voice said, "Jacob, if he is to be saved by us, it must come through you. Now!"

Jacob closed his eyes and concentrated. He felt an odd vibration—not in his ghostly form, but in some connection to the temporal world—the first he had felt since he had left his mortal form just steps from where he now stood. Real, earthly life was not within his grasp, but he somehow could draw near to it, to send small tendrils of feeling into it. He felt his presence fill the house. He could see, through his eyelids, Scrooge sitting before the fire in his apartment. Jacob once again saw Scrooge, this time from the vantage point of standing right in the hearth, staring out at him.

Again, Scrooge looked up and seemed to notice him. No fear was in his visage, however—only cynical doubt. Scrooge eventually turned from Jacob's gaze, concentrating his efforts on his lukewarm gruel. The vision faded, and when Jacob opened his eyes, he was still at the foot of the stairs.

Throwing his heart into another, greater effort, he closed his eyes and said, "Spirit, you have brought me here. I know you would not have done so without there being a way. Spirit, I want to help Ebenezer. Please give me power to do so!"

With that, a noise began. Somewhere in the house, a bell began to tinkle, then ring, then nearly shake with anxiety. It was joined by other bells. Parlor bells for announcing guests. Kitchen bells for calling a meal. Other bells, thickly laden with the dust of years separating them from their long-lost purpose, all pealed, without organization or pattern, each bell giving whatever power it had to the grand announcement of a change in spirit of this home.

"Jacob," the spirit said softly, "you are ready. He is ready. Go."

Jacob began to walk up the stairs. It was not his walk of all the past years, but a human walk. He was not restored to humanity, but he had an essence of it. His chains clanked, and he could hear for the first time an echo from their protestations. This was not the otherworldly sound, noticeable only to Jacob, to punish him in its reminder of his deeds. This was real sound, life sound, the reverberations of real things in real places. As he walked, the chains' weight was no less real. It may even have been greater than if he had pulled them in life, but Jacob set his mind on his sole purpose: to ascend those stairs, to confront Scrooge, and to warn him of his self-imposed impending doom.

He saw the light coming from under the door of Scrooge's room. He slowly shuffled toward it. As he was not released from his fate as a spirit, he slowly walked right through the door. He looked at Scrooge, Scrooge at him, and there was no doubt he was seen.

There is no laughter, no joy in the realm in which Marley served his time, and these joys were equally missing in Scrooge's home. In fact, there was a great deal of similarity between the two environments. But if there were a space for humor in the dark apartment, this was it. When Scrooge noticed Marley, his face became a museum display of every possible derivation of human emotion surrounding the cousins of disbelief and fear. His eyebrows surged up and down; his breathing sped, then stopped, then sped again; his eyes widened in surprise, narrowed in confusion, widened in fear, and narrowed in suspicion of this unknown visitor. It was as though his face were inhabited by some unknown creature that raced around beneath his skin manipulating every muscle and joint in his head.

Gathering his senses, Scrooge asked, "How now! What do you want with me?" seeming more annoyed than surprised.

"Much!" Marley responded, feeling shock as he heard his own voice echo off the walls of the room.

It shook Scrooge in its otherworldly tone. Again, he seemed to force his emotions back into check. "Who are you?" Scrooge asked with a practiced hardness.

"Ask me who I was," Jacob replied mournfully.

"Who were you then? You're particular, for a shade."

"In life I was your partner, Jacob Marley."

Scrooge contemplated this, seeming agitated at first. But as he had done so many times, he placed that which bothered him in a context that allowed him to discard it. He dealt with the apparition by deciding it was not in fact an apparition but a figment of his imagination.

When Marley heard this he could not stop himself from sobbing the mournful call that had been his script since his passing. The pain welled up and out of him, fairly dousing Scrooge.

"Mercy!" Scrooge cried. "Dreadful apparition, why do you trouble me?"

Marley told Scrooge of his fate since his death. He showed him the chains and told of their origin, how he had forged each link with some assault on humankind.

Marley saw the fear in Scrooge's heart, but Scrooge's fear was of the ghost of Marley, not of the effects of his own misguided life. Marley told him of the chain he, Scrooge, actually bore, as heavy as Marley's was years ago. Scrooge did not believe him as he looked about for it, but vaguely, mistily, Jacob saw it. It was not yet a burden to Scrooge, but it lay in wait like vipers positioning for the kill, its iron clasps ready to shut upon his wrists and ankles.

Scrooge heard Marley's lament, the weight of his sad testimony of opportunity lost surrounding them as a whirlwind. But he could not reconcile this punishment for a man who had worked so hard. "But you were always a good man of business, Jacob!"

The contradiction heightened Jacob's pain. *Business.* The way he had gone about business had soured him on the word. To Scrooge, he bore solemn testimony of the misuse of his gifts. "Business! Mankind was my business. The common welfare was my business; charity, mercy, forbearance, and benevolence, were, all, my business. The dealings of my trade were but a drop of water in the comprehensive ocean of my business!" He raised his chains, then threw them against the ground, as if to shake off all he had done. This final act seemed to cause Scrooge to begin to shake.

"Hear me!" Jacob said forcefully and solemnly. "My time is almost gone."

With that, Marley saw what was going to happen. It was as though time ceased to be a sequential thing but instead was like pages in a book, torn out and pasted upon the wall, for Marley to peruse at once. He did not see the spirits themselves, but he knew what would be the sequence of coming events and what he needed to say.

"You will be haunted," Marley said, "by three Spirits."

Scrooge protested, but Marley ignored him. "Without

their visits," he warned, "you cannot hope to shun the path I tread. Expect the first to-morrow, when the bell tolls one. Expect the second on the next night at the same hour. The third upon the next night when the last stroke of twelve has ceased to vibrate. Look to see me no more; and look that, for your own sake, you remember what has passed between us!" Jacob did not tell Ebenezer, for it was not his to tell, that if he did not heed each spirit, then his life would end.

Marley felt the brief connection with this world begin to fade. The wanderings were pulling him in. His experience told him this was a struggle he could not win, and his only outcome was to give up and die again as he fell within its grasp. The sounds of the tormented began to rise again in his consciousness, and he was grateful at least for the brief respite in which they had been silenced to his ghostly ears.

One last thought struck him. He had lost the ability to speak to Scrooge any more, but he beckoned to him, drawing him to the window.

Scrooge approached carefully, and if he was not devoid of color in his face already, this drained the last of it. The sounds of the condemned spirits, passing in their dreadful parade, wafted into the room, and Scrooge both heard their cries and saw their fruitless attempts to help even those on the street below his sill who had no idea of their presence.

Marley fell backward into the fray, watching Scrooge at the window staring in horror at the scene. He said to himself, "Listen to them, oh man, listen and hear."

He then raised his voice in the song of agony and turned toward his next destination.

8

Jacob Marley wearily looked to see the next testimonial of his wasted life. But, to his surprise, he was not traversing the earth. He was back in Scrooge's bedchamber. He heard the church nearby peal the hour. Never had a single chime sounded with so much vibrancy, so much importance, and the potential of so much dread.

At once, light seemed to fill the room. Jacob was standing by the door when, between him and Scrooge, a man of pure white appeared. Marley was long past starting in surprise at spirits, but this one was unique. He was pure and perfect in form like a child, yet carried himself in confidence and wisdom like an old man. His hair was flawless white but his skin was smooth and young; his musculature strong and developed, but his carriage unassuming. His clothing and all his adornments were white, save for a rim of summer flowers about the hem of his robe and the single sprig of holly he held in his hand.

"Spirit!" was all Jacob could mutter.

"Jacob, you did your part well." Though the spirit was there, he still communicated with Marley through his thoughts. "We will see if Scrooge receives me. If he uses his logic to force me out, we will be done before we begin."

The spirit raised the curtains of Scrooge's bed although his hands remained serenely clasped before him, pinching a tall cap beneath his arm. Scrooge and Marley both stared at the apparition. From the top of the spirit's head, light poured forth. It felt to Jacob as if he had been in a winter storm until he could no longer feel his hands and feet, and then entered an inn to confront a roaring hearth. The warmth was rich upon him, yet at the same time it pained his skin as it melted his frostbite.

Scrooge was staring oddly at the ghost.

"What is it, Spirit?" Jacob asked.

"He does not accept me. My image is fading in and out of his perception. I fear . . ."

Scrooge could not see or hear Marley. Marley shared

the room with these two personages but was of the sphere of neither of them. He was not mortal like Scrooge, and therefore could not make connection with him, and he was not divine like the spirit, so could not enter the stage to make himself visible to Scrooge.

Scrooge seemed to look more deeply at the spirit.

"Ah, now he sees me," Marley heard from the spirit.

Scrooge addressed the ghost fearfully. "Are you the Spirit, sir, whose coming was foretold to me?" asked Scrooge.

"I am!" the spirit replied with a soft but firm voice.

"Who, and what are you?" Scrooge demanded.

"I am the Ghost of Christmas Past."

The spirit was able to talk openly with Scrooge, while still talking through his thoughts to the unseen Marley.

"Rise!" the spirit commanded. "And walk with me."

They moved toward the window, and as Scrooge took the hand of the Ghost of Christmas Past, the three of them were standing in an instant in the country. It was not a picture of the country, it was the country. The smells and sounds permeated their consciousness.

"This place," Marley asked the ghost, "was this his home?"

"It was. Scrooge grew up among these fields and lanes."

Then they were in a schoolroom where a lone student sat reading.

"Is that Ebenezer?" Jacob asked.

"It is."

"Why is he alone?"

"Because he is not wanted in his home. He is left here, on this Christmas as on others, to be by himself. He reads, and his imagination keeps him company, but it is a wall built against the hurt of not being loved in his family. It sustains him but is a poor substitute for the loving cradle of a mother's arm, or a father's praise for growing well."

Jacob had had no idea. Scrooge had not shared one word about his youth in all the years they had worked together. Seeing the contrast to his own growing up, wherein Jacob had been surrounded by the care of parents and the love and companionship of siblings, his heart was seared with pain for Scrooge's lack of even a semblance of the same.

While Scrooge and the Ghost of Christmas Past talked of the scene, Jacob thought of the chances he had possessed to keep those relationships alive, and how he had snuffed them out with vigor. At the end of his life, he had had no idea whether his siblings lived or died. But, in his wanderings since his death, he had seen them. They had married, had families and grandchildren, and lived the kind of lives he and they had lived as children. But, in each one, there was a hole Jacob had drilled with his absence and lined against refilling. His mere lack of presence had hurt them all.

"Why is he not loved? Is he a bad child?" Jacob asked.

"No child is bad, Jacob. His father lost his wife early in their years together. Scrooge's only crime was that he reminded his father of her. He put Scrooge in this school to push away the painful memories of the one he lost."

Marley heard Scrooge speak. "I wish," Scrooge muttered, putting his hand in his pocket and looking about him, after drying his eyes with his cuff, "but it's too late now."

"What is the matter?" asked the spirit.

"Nothing," said Scrooge. "Nothing. There was a boy singing a Christmas carol at my door last night. I should like to have given him something: that's all."

The spirit turned toward Jacob and offered the faintest hint of a smile.

With that, the scene changed again. They were in the

same locale, but it was a few years later, a fact made notice-able by the unglamorous, ungentle aging of the school but more so by the growth of the young boy. He stood now a teen.

A young girl, small and delicate but as strong in her resolve as she seemed vulnerable in her form, ran into the room and hugged the youthful Scrooge, calling him "dear brother."

"Spirit," Jacob exclaimed, "I know this girl. Who is she?"

"You are quite a woman, little Fan," the memory of Scrooge said as if in direct answer to Jacob's question.

"Fan, Fan, Fan," Jacob wondered. Suddenly, an echo from a brief moment in time many years ago filled his mind, and with it came a profound foreboding. In the driving snow, a young man gingerly placed a pregnant woman on the seat box of a cart. He urged her to hold tight, to protect herself and her soon-to-be-born child. Their image dimmed quickly, just as it had when Marley had ignored the needs of the couple that day. But he heard, as he had heard then, the caring husband call her by name.

Marley's voice started to crack as he asked, "Spirit, I dare not query you on this, for I fear the answer it brings, but is this Fan the same Fan I evicted with her husband from the home I managed?"

"Yes, she is the same."

Again his mind revealed a picture from his past, framed with darkness. He was in his carriage, frustrated, and walking next to him was a young Scrooge. Now doing his best to suppress the rising emotion, Marley continued, "And, Spirit, this Fan—is she the one whose funeral parade I followed the day I met Ebenezer?"

"Yes," the ghost said matter-of-factly, "this little girl is that woman who was ready to bear a child herself."

Jacob's voice shook harder. "So, Spirit, she had the child, who grew to be the nephew who showed so much kindness to Scrooge, and then she died?"

"She did."

"What caused her death?" Jacob whispered.

"Why, she caused her own death, of course," the spirit replied. "They got into a home they should have known they could not afford. They should have known he would lose his employment. They should have looked at the calendar and considered all these things when they decided to bring God's most precious gift into the world. I would not worry, Jacob—her death was none of your affair."

"But it was my affair . . ."

The spirit turned to him and addressed him sharply. "Do you know what you could have been to Fan and John?"

"I do now."

"You do not!" the spirit said with as much force as it had said anything to this point. It was not anger, but righteous indignation. "You will yet see, and then you will know."

Jacob was rebuffed by the spirit's firmness. Carefully he asked, "Why is she here, in this place, today, with Scrooge?"

"Their father is willing, thanks to the pleading of this loving girl, to take Ebenezer back into their home. Yet the father will not be close to the boy, will not share all the gifts only a father can give his child."

"As my father did with me."

"Yes, as Joseph did with you. And as you may have shared with Ebenezer when he came into your partnership."

"As a father? What father might I have been to Scrooge?" Jacob asked incredulously and with some degree of accusation. "He was a man, as I was. What fatherly gifts could I have given him?"

"What gifts did you prize from your father?"

Jacob looked into the mists that surrounded them. "His love and counsel. His support. His correction with compassion."

"Was Ebenezer so old that he was not in need of love and counsel, support, and correction with compassion?"

Jacob looked sorrowful. "No, he was not, as I am not. That is what I have gotten from the spirits. Was I supposed to give this to Scrooge?"

"It was one reason your paths crossed. But you buried those gifts. You forced them from your life. They were yours to give, but you made certain that they were given to no man."

The dialogue between Scrooge and the ghost continued, Marley mostly quiet, hoping for Scrooge to yield to its presentations.

Again they traveled to a new time and place. They were in a warehouse, not unlike Marley's in its purpose and design, but unlike it in every other conceivable way. It was bright and happy and bedecked in Christmas decorations. There were gaily dressed girls dancing with sharp young boys who vied for their attention. A feast was spread, offering a bounteous harvest second only to the abundance of merry wishes, laughs, and good cheer among the participants. Scrooge appeared to be engaged in all the activities, losing his recognition that he was just a spectator.

A fiddler was playing "Sir Roger de Coverley," and the entire room was reeling in an attempt to carry out the dance, the dancers bumping into each other in their mistakes and making it all the merrier by laughing at their own shortcomings. From the crowd emerged an older couple, dancing to the delight of everyone else. They moved as one, not so much in their perfect dance—though it was so when compared with all the others in the room—but in their harmony as a couple, which caused both their talent and their errors to refine them somehow into one beautiful whole. In fact, they glowed, quite literally, lighting the faces of all those in the room, and though nobody else could see the luminance, they all benefited from it.

"Who is that?" Jacob asked.

"Mr. and Mrs. Fezziwig. The man runs this countinghouse. His profession is yours." The contrast between himself and Fezziwig was not lost on Marley. His countinghouse had never looked like this, never was a place of joy.

"Why does he glow with his wife?" Marley asked.

"He is a complete man," the spirit said, with obvious admiration for Fezziwig. "Not a perfect man, but perfect in his desires. He loves his wife with all his soul. His heart never forgets a prayer for his children. He treats those he employs with care. Look about, Jacob. See who is here. The men of high station from his clientele, and the workers of his business, and their friends, and their friends. They are all friends to Fezziwig. He has no regard for their position, but for the only position that matters to him: that they are fellow sojourners on this earth. For Fezziwig, that is enough to make him open his doors and share his good fortune with all who may need it."

Marley thought about how, in all the years he had employed Duffin, he had not once given him so much as a Christmas roll. When Duffin left the countinghouse each day, Marley did not know where he went, to whom he went, or what cares or concerns he took with him. Did he dance with a wife? Did he counsel with his children, or bounce his grandchildren on his lap? Did he sit alone? Marley had no idea.

The spirit shook him from his thought, saying abruptly, "My time grows short. Quick!"

They had moved forward some number of Christmases. Scrooge looked exactly as he had the day Marley had met him. He sat on a bench with a beautiful young woman, who had been crying. The old Scrooge knew this moment, and he and the girl seemed united in the grief caused them both by this younger Scrooge.

Jacob knew this scene too, not from any recognition of the surroundings, but from the conflict that was playing out. He had never met the woman, nor had the spirit told him a thing, but he had contributed to this occurring, and, upon seeing it, immediately dreaded it.

The young woman addressed Ebenezer. "Another idol has displaced me; and if it can cheer and comfort you in time to come, as I would have tried to do, I have no just cause to grieve."

"What idol has displaced you?" he rejoined.

"A golden one."

"This is the even-handed dealing of the world!" he said. "There is nothing on which it is so hard as poverty; and there is nothing it professes to condemn with such severity as the pursuit of wealth!"

Jacob shuddered and felt as if he would explode. "This counsel was mine," he mourned.

The spirit sensed his anguish and said, "They were his words spoken, not yours."

"Yes, Spirit, but I said them to him just days before this meeting. I gave them to him."

"He must make his own decisions."

"Yes, but this was my wisdom, my twisted perception of how the world worked. Had I not said anything, might he have remained betrothed?"

"Perhaps, but it is unknown. The past is gone. These are shadows of what already has been."

For all his ache, Jacob momentarily forgot the pain as he looked at Scrooge. From his vantage point, he had a silhouette of the old Scrooge's profile, whose eyes fairly begged his former self to stop. Tears flowed freely down his cheeks. His head shook, accepting his inability to change what he saw, and mourning his own mistakes. If love was one of the most powerful things Jacob had felt, then love lost, especially at one's own hand, must be the most painful.

The spirit and Marley sadly looked with Scrooge upon the final moments of this encounter. The beautiful young woman spoke:

"I release you. With a full heart, for the love of him you once were. You may—the memory of what is past half makes me hope you will—have pain in this. A very, very brief time, and you will dismiss the recollection of it, gladly, as an unprofitable dream, from which it happened well that you awoke. May you be happy in the life you have chosen!"

"No," Jacob yelled at the image of the younger Scrooge and losing himself in the moment. "Go after her, plead for her forgiveness. Do what you must to earn back her trust. You fool, do not let her go!"

But, of course, these were just shadows of the past, and the Scrooge of so many years ago did just what he had done then. He stood still as she left. Marley turned back to the twosome, who stared through him at the departing image of Belle. While the Scrooge of the present stood stonily, Marley cried the ghostly tears that accompanied his condition. He thought he saw luminescent tears running down the cheeks of Christmas Past.

Scrooge begged the ghost to take him home, but the spirit persisted, escorting them again to a new time and place.

The scene changed. They were with Belle again, but the years had passed and she was a mother several times over. Her children flowed like a river around her, to her complete joy and delight. Shortly, the man who had become her husband entered the room. When the children finished swarming him, to which he returned every one a kiss, he made a comment to his wife.

"Belle," said the husband, seeming a bit excited to

share an intrigue, "I saw an old friend of yours this after-noon."

"Who was it?"

"Guess!"

"How can I? Tut, don't I know?" and making a joke of it, she said, "Mr. Scrooge."

"Mr. Scrooge it was. I passed his office window; and as it was not shut up, and he had a candle inside, I could scarcely help seeing him. His partner lies upon the point of death, I hear; and there he sat alone. Quite alone in the world, I do believe."

"Was it not an odd coincidence," the spirit said to Jacob, "that Belle's husband happened to walk by the countinghouse, that he happened to look inside at a time Scrooge was there, and that it happened to occur on the day you died?"

"Spirit, I am no longer a believer in coincidence," Jacob confessed.

The spirit looked back at the home. "This man might have stopped, rather than run home to tell his wife of the loneliness of Scrooge. He might have entered the count-inghouse and said, 'Excuse me, Mr. Scrooge. I have heard of the impending loss of your partner. I just want to give you my condolences.' What do you think would have happened then, Jacob?"

"Ebenezer would have chased him out with a rod?"

The spirit nodded, "He might have. But he also might have thought, 'Who is this man who needs nothing from me, but only wishes me comfort?' He might not have changed that moment, but that experience might have worked within him.

"But, we shall not know. For the man's sole aim was to tell Belle of the plight of her former fiancé and appear to take no small delight in it." The spirit turned away. "There is yet one more scene. Jacob, this one is for you alone to see."

The ghost and Jacob stood in an alleyway. It was dark, and only two things permeated the space. Small shafts of light from the lamps on the street shone in just enough to illuminate the scene, and wind—cold, biting, unforgiving wind—managed to work its way from whatever openings existed above to fill this space with the worst possible atmosphere. Rubbish lay along the sides of the alley where the path met the walls of a house. Within, some family warmed themselves, oblivious to what lay in the shade of the bricks that separated them by just a few feet.

"Come with me," the spirit said, and they walked

along the uneven stones, brushing past discarded trash and boxes and rags. Here and there, small fires had been set in old pots, and around them, figures huddled, straining to extract warmth from the weak flames. The dress of these people was as gray as the surroundings, and they seemed to be an extension of the lifelessness of the place.

The spirit stopped and looked down upon what Jacob at first thought was a particularly large pile of garbage, but when he focused, he saw it was a couple. The woman sat on the ground, leaning against the wall. A man crouched by her, attempting to shield her from the wind and snow. Her head lolled, too heavy for her to support upright. But from her face radiated a light. Whether it was reflected or actually came from within her, Jacob did not know, but it defied the situation in which she found herself.

As the husband reached up to adjust a blanket about her, Jacob saw for the first time that in her arms there was a child, an infant. All that was visible were two eyes and a tiny pink nose. Despite the condition of the woman, she looked lovingly upon the bundle. The man smoothed the blanket and then wiped his cheek before placing his arm back around his wife's head to comfort her.

"Fan, he is beautiful," the man said, his words broken by his emotions. "He has your features, your grace, and your strength." He now cried more openly and laid his head on hers. "Fan, all the days of his life, I will look into his eyes and see you, and miss you, with all my heart."

"Do you know these people, Jacob?" the spirit asked.

Jacob did not answer. He had fallen to his knees, trying ineffectually to ward off the weather by spreading his arms around the trio. He wanted to offer warmth, but coldness was his constitution and he had none to give.

Fan looked up at John. "Please take him, John, I cannot hold him anymore." John carefully placed the wrapped baby against his chest with one arm while he pulled Fan closer with the other. She spoke, with great effort and haltingly. "John, take care of our little Fred. You are and will be a good father." She swallowed. "And John, you are all I ever hoped for. I will love you forever. Thank you for loving me."

With ever so slight and gentle a movement, she moved closer to John and then closed her eyes as she passed from life.

"Oh, Fan!" John cried out. "Fan, Fan. I am sorry I could not protect you. Fan, Fan, Fan." He wept against his wife's still form.

"Spirit, I killed this woman," Jacob sobbed. He turned his head up to look at the spirit. "I killed her. I alone had the power to give her a place to have this child. It would have taken just a small act of kindness to give this woman life, this child a mother, this man his wife. But, no, I wanted my rent." He could barely get the words out.

"At least you have her pearl," the spirit said flatly.

"Spirit!" he yelled out. "Do you not think I have learned anything in these woeful years? Don't you realize that pearl is a symbol of my complete corruption, which I can now do nothing about? Forgive me for speaking to you so sharply, but have you no compassion? Do you think I do not understand why we are here? Do you think I would keep that pearl, and have that child not have a mother, were I to be able to relive this time?"

"You did not kill her, Jacob," the spirit comforted him. "She was always a frail woman. Even if she had been in the house, she might yet have died."

"But even then, I might have given her a final comfort before she died, a place to pass where her husband might mourn her privately. Where family might have gathered to comfort each other. I had that power! If we do nothing but to remove a rock upon which someone might have tripped, though they may never know we did it, is this not our cause, our reason for life? Oh, Spirit, I was a wretched man."

Jacob leaned forward, head almost touching the ground before John. Covering his face with his hands, he sobbed.

The spirit placed his hand on Marley's shoulder. He gently drew him back to a standing position and moved him back. A few women, dressed in similarly gray and ragged clothing, surrounded Fan and added their cries to the heartless alley. A man squatted by John and put his arm around his shoulder. John laid his head against the man's shoulder and cried with abandon.

Jacob could only shake his head and share the sorrow with these unknown, unfortunate paupers in an unknown alley in an unknown part of town.

The Ghost of Christmas Past patted him with care and said softly, "Now, Jacob, you understand."

Suddenly they were back at Belle's home with Scrooge, who had been watching the woman who might have been his wife. Scrooge turned to look at the spirit in anger. Throughout these visits, Scrooge had seemed to be softening, showing an emotion Jacob had never observed in him. With each scene of the past, the frost upon Scrooge's soul was melting. But, for Scrooge, this had been too much. He grabbed the cap that the spirit had carried the entire time. Though Scrooge came at him with aggression, the spirit stood calmly and did not resist. The light from the top of his head seemed a great offense to Scrooge, and he slapped the hat upon the spirit and forced it down, attempting to extinguish the light that so bothered his conscience.

Marley looked on in sadness. The entire spirit was fully shrouded by the hat but for a thin rim of light that could not be contained. Drawing close to understanding, Scrooge could not face his reality. He had darkened the one light that represented a chance for him.

Then, everything around Jacob became dark. Scrooge was gone. The spirit was gone.

"Spirit?" Jacob called hesitantly.

He heard a voice, a new one.

"Jacob, it is time to visit with Scrooge again. Come now."

9

Once again, Marley was in Scrooge's home, this time in the drawing room next to the bedroom. He was startled to see what appeared to be the entire fruit and vegetable market from Cornhill spread across the chair, the table, and the floor. Jacob had not been aware that so much color even existed. In his gray little world and his gray little life, he had missed this variety. In the midst of the bounty sat a new spirit. His form was large, his hair rich and full.

As Marley was taking it in, he heard the spirit bellow, "Come in! Come in! And get to know me better, man!"

The door between the bedchamber and the drawing room opened slowly, with Scrooge's nightcap first emerging in the widening crack, followed by his forehead, then his eyes, which, like Jacob's, were wide with surprise. In awe, he shuffled into the room, seeming quite off guard. The more surprised he looked, the more the spirit seemed to enjoy it, and he put back his head and laughed a belly laugh that almost commanded Jacob to smile.

Jacob was surveying the harvest when the spirit said to Scrooge in a deep, resonating voice, "I am the Ghost of Christmas Present. Look upon me."

Scrooge did. And Jacob did. And they both seemed to see that, with their gaze, the room was yet even more full.

Scrooge reached out to touch the robe of the spirit and, in not even a blink, for one could not have shut and opened an eye in the time it took for the transition, they were standing on the street. Jacob had been thus transported along with the spirit and Ebenezer.

They were in the marketplace on Christmas morning. Shops and racks filled with meats and vegetables and fruits of every kind, from every reach of England and the world, were the object of the crowds of people. Those thronging the markets were bidding each other a Merry Christmas in the happiest of ways and selecting their foods for Christmas dinner. The cold notwithstanding, the crowds brought their own warmth in their pleasant bumpings against one another.

If anyone had had the vision to see these three spirit visitors, the trio would have made quite a sight: Scrooge wearing his slippers, bedclothes, and nightcap; Marley dressed in his aging waistcoat, head bound up with his death scarf, wound with chains from which bounced his eternal collection of cash boxes, locks, and keys; and the two of them flanking the giant spirit, bedecked in his green robes, bare chest clearly feeling no pain of cold, brown ringlets of hair flowing down his shoulders, and head topped with a crown of holly. But it was only Jacob and the spirit who saw it all, for Scrooge had no idea of Marley's presence, and nobody on the street had a sense of any of the three of them.

Except, occasionally, for a child.

At that moment, an urchin of no more than five stood before the trio. Whether she could not see Marley and Scrooge, or whether she simply paid them no mind, it could not be discerned, but there was no question she saw the ghost, as she surveyed his entire wardrobe and stared with delight into his face. The spirit smiled down at her. He took his cornucopia torch and tipped it above her head, which caused a soundless waterfall of glistening sparkles, like a thousand miniature sprites, that seemed to flow into the girl as they touched her.

"Spirit," asked Jacob, "why does she see you?"

"I cannot stop her. It is not that I choose to reveal myself to her, but I am revealed by her purity. She sees me because her eyes are not shrouded with doubt or hate, fear or selfishness or greed. Her heart is innocent, and her eyes are an extension of that heart. My mission is the goodness of man in this season, and I cannot keep it from her."

"Do all the children see you?"

"No, just the ones whose spirits are so remarkable, they tend to live in both worlds."

"And what is that with which you christened her?"

"Joy, that it might fill her needs a bit."

Marley seemed troubled. "She does not look like she needs joy. I think she needs food—and clothing."

"Look about you," said the spirit more sternly. "Do you see food?"

Marley again took in the array of fruits and vegetables and nuts and plants of all kinds. "I do, Spirit. So much that to feed this little one even all she could swallow would not make a noticeable scratch on this abundance."

"And do you see people?"

There were men and women and children bustling about, wishing each other the greatest merriment of the day and generally enjoying the morning.

"I do, Spirit, many."

"And what number of that many are stooping down to offer one bite, or perhaps an old shawl they would never miss, to this poor girl?"

Jacob noticed that the crowds seemed completely oblivious to the child, walking around her and even bumping her at times, looking down only to see what inconvenience they had stepped on and, upon finding it to be only an urchin girl, looking back up to continue their conversations, never missing a word.

"None," Jacob confessed. "Not one seems to notice her."

"They all could, Jacob, if they chose. But they seem not to care. So, in this, I provide a little to give her what they may not."

"But if she is hungry, why not give her all she needs?"

"Do not think that a spirit does not have a kind heart! For we do. I ache for her needs. But if I were to give her food and clothing and a home, what would be required of you?"

Marley looked upon the girl, who returned the

sprinkling with a smile and then, despite her condition, skipped off into the crowd.

Scrooge had continued to survey the scene, wide-eyed, oblivious to the young girl's interaction with the Ghost of Christmas Present.

"Spirit," Marley asked, changing his tone, "is this the morning of Christmas?"

"It is."

"The one that comes after Christmas Eve?"

The spirit shook as he laughed. "The same. Is there another I am not privy to? Am I not attendant to my duty?"

"No, of course. I know that there is only one Christmas a year, after the eve. But this should be the day after Christmas, not Christmas Day. Your spirits, your brethren, they said that they would come each on one of three successive nights. The Ghost of Christmas Past came on Christmas morning. Yet *this* is Christmas morning."

The spirit, who to this point had fairly radiated the warmth of humor and joy, had a small twinge of soberness in his voice. "Ebenezer's time is very short," he said. "Three days would extend us past his hour."

"But, Spirit, your kindred said that if Ebenezer turned

from his ways, if he embraced the kindness that he and I so defiantly dismissed our entire lives, if he would taste and give of love, he might extend his time."

"But it appears he did not. We now come in one night to give him as much chance as possible."

"I saw him visit his past. I saw him weep—"

The spirit cut him off sharply. "Weep! Weep for what, Jacob?"

Jacob was taken aback. "Why, for his loss, for what might have been! I have never seen him show one bit of emotion in my life."

"Jacob, all the souls that drift in your sphere of punishment weep for what might have been. True, he feels sorrow, and from sorrow can spring change. But if his sorrow does not become resolve, and his resolve give birth to action, then his lot has not changed. You saw him try to extinguish the light of Christmas Past. He did as he has done most of his life. He has tried to put out the light and, finding it insufferable, he has covered it."

Jacob was silent. One day for Ebenezer to change. He had considered it a bit naïve to think that three days after a lifetime of avarice should be enough, but whatever value there had been in that span, it was now two days shorter.

They left the market and next were upon the step of

the Cratchit home. Before entering, the spirit again tipped his horn, as he had been doing their short but entire journey, and dusted the lintel of the door with blessings.

"Your horn must nearly be empty."

The ghost looked at Marley with an impish smile, then looked inside in mock concern. With a *hmmm*, he turned it slightly toward Marley, who could see it teeming with light. "See, it's full," the spirit said.

Marley just looked at him, so the spirit continued. "Endless, Jacob."

Entering the Cratchit home, the three of them stepped into the midst of an unrestrained harmony of Christmas celebration. Jacob's head whipped back and forth as children ran about him.

Through the front door and into the happy mayhem stepped Bob Cratchit, bearing on his back his rider, a small lad with a brace upon his leg. There was a great deal of celebration as everyone greeted one another in such a way as to cause a person to wonder if they had not been gone a season rather than an hour.

The young lame boy intrigued Jacob, and he seemed to intrigue Scrooge as well. He was clearly crippled, yet no less joy shone in his face than in the countenances of any of the full-bodied children who carried him to another room.

Mrs. Cratchit drew close to her husband. "And how did little Tim behave?" she asked.

"As good as gold," said Bob, "and better. Somehow he gets thoughtful, sitting by himself so much, and thinks the strangest things you ever heard. He told me, coming home, that he hoped the people saw him in the church, because he was a cripple, and it might be pleasant to them to remember upon Christmas Day, who made lame beggars walk, and blind men see."

"And they did, Jacob," said the spirit, turning to him with a smile. "They did. There were a few hearts, persuaded by different and unique circumstances, who were in church this morning. Many saw Tim. Some felt sorry for him. Some," he sighed, "as is the case with your kind, wondered what evil the boy had done, or perhaps his parents, that the child might be marked by his infirmity. But a few in that church, seeing the boy not just walk out on his crutch, but walk out bearing the countenance of an angel, turned back to their own troubles with new perspective."

In his lifetime, Marley had seen the architectural wonder of the Cathedral Church of Paul the Apostle. He had marveled at the ships built in his native town, of so great a mass that he could not lift a single timber used in the hull, yet they danced in the water when launched. He had seen business arrangements so artful in their complexity that only a few minds could even comprehend them. And yet, for all the majesty of the creations of brilliant men, he felt, this moment, that he had never seen anything so masterful, so complete, so elegant as the unity of this little poor family in this nondescript home in Camden Town. His entire life, he had marveled with disapproval at how the destitute allowed life to assault them. Yet this, here, this alone was life! This was the heartbeat for which the rest of the world existed.

There was a dance being performed here. To the untrained, it looked tumultuous and unconcerned. But within the dance, Marley saw a rhythm to which all the dancers responded. It moved between them and unified them.

Scrooge spoke to the Ghost of Christmas Present. "Spirit," he said, "tell me if Tiny Tim will live."

"I see a vacant seat," replied the Ghost, "in the poor chimney-corner, and a crutch without an owner, carefully preserved. If these shadows remain unaltered by the Future, the child will die."

"No, no," said Scrooge. "Oh, no, kind Spirit! Say he will be spared."

"If these shadows remain unaltered by the Future, none other of my race will find him here," returned the Ghost. "What then? If he be like to die, he had better do it, and decrease the surplus population."

"Scrooge can help this boy, Spirit," Jacob said enthusiastically.

"He may," the spirit said sadly, "but I fear he most likely will not. The boy's time is also short."

"Can't someone else do something?" Marley asked. "Might some other so moved by this boy take up his cause?"

"No," the kindly spirit said. "This opportunity is for Scrooge alone to fulfill. Nobody can replace the role he has in this short life to help Tiny Tim."

"But, what if he does not?" cried Marley. "Certainly you cannot condemn the boy for the lost soul of Scrooge. For in Scrooge's living of his days, if he misses this one sign, why should the boy lose his life? There is no justice to it!"

"Justice?" said the ghost. "Jacob, if the actions of man did not matter, if spirits removed every obstacle from life, would you not blame every success your neighbor won and every failure you bore as the random or unfair decisions of a race you could not see? 'Why,' you would ask, 'does this one live and this one die?' And all the while they were doing so, you would do nothing for them, pondering your grand misfortune for not being smiled upon rather than using your liberty to change the course of events. Jacob, this choice you have is a gift, and we must let you use it, for good or ill."

This did not satisfy Marley. "But can there not be another for whom the experience of helping Tiny Tim might be important?"

"In this case, these two paths were meant to cross, and, on this issue, they alone."

Jacob was rebuked and looked with pity and frustration upon the boy. "As with Fan," he said under his breath.

"As with Fan," the spirit confirmed.

They stood in silence another moment. Suddenly the spirit said, "My time grows short."

Jacob reared back as he looked at the spirit's robes, as did Scrooge when he too noticed the fearful sight.

"Forgive me if I am not justified in what I ask," said Scrooge, looking intently at the spirit's robe, "but I see something strange, and not belonging to yourself, protruding from your skirts. Is it a foot or a claw?"

"It might be a claw, for the flesh there is upon it," was the spirit's sorrowful reply. "Look here."

The spirit parted the bottom of his robe and two children emerged. These were not joyous and bright like the Cratchit children, even Tiny Tim with his infirmity. These were dark and empty and lost.

"Oh, Man! Look down here!" exclaimed the Ghost.

"Spirit," thought Jacob, repulsed by the sordid sight, "why do you allow these children to be like this?"

"Why do you?" answered back the spirit in thought.

To both Scrooge and Marley, he said, "They cling to me, appealing from their fathers. This boy is Ignorance. This girl is Want. Beware them both, and all of their degree, but most of all beware this boy, for on his brow I see that written which is Doom, unless the writing be erased. Deny it!" cried the spirit, stretching out its hand toward the city. "Slander those who tell it ye! Admit it for your factious purposes, and make it worse. And bide the end!"

Scrooge was horrified, but Jacob stood transfixed. "Ignorance and Want," he said to himself.

"Yes," the spirit said to him. "You know them both. You played upon these two frailties of man. You took advantage of want. You knew that for people to fall into your design, their human demands must be unmet, and in that state, they were more vulnerable. Once there, you then took advantage of their ignorance. Your lofty knowledge, your fine mind—you used these things as a bludgeon to beat your fellow man into submission.

"You lament that your choices left you no family. You do have family, both you and Scrooge. These are the children you have born and bred. They are what you invested in. They are your true legacy."

As Jacob stared upon the children, from his consciousness, he heard the striking of a clock, his clock—Scrooge's clock—and the grand old spirit of the present appeared to wither and disappear.

Marley looked at Scrooge, who was looking up in horror. Marley followed his gaze. Laid before his eyes was an apparition of complete fearfulness.

10

The tall, hooded figure approached them and pointed out into the shadows.

"Am I in the presence of the Ghost of Christmas Yet to Come?" Scrooge asked fearfully.

The hooded phantom nodded. Scrooge was terrified.

"Ghost of the Future!" he exclaimed, "I fear you more than any spectre I have seen. But as I know your purpose is to do me good, and as I hope to live to be another man from what I was, I am prepared to bear you company, and do it with a thankful heart. Will you not speak to me?"

The ghost continued to point.

"Jacob," Marley heard a voice say.

"Spirit, you speak to me and not Scrooge?"

"I speak to you both. But Ebenezer does not hear. This night, his shred of faith in our existence has permitted him to abide our presence. But now, his fear defines his vision."

"Fear of you, then," Jacob said.

"Fear of what I represent," answered the spirit.

"But you come in such an image," Jacob pointed out. "It seems you intend to bring fear in your wake."

"You see me as you see death. To another, for whom death represents the conclusion of a happy sum of goodly days on the earth, this is not my appearance. My appearance is of your making, not mine."

Scrooge and Marley followed the spirit as throughout the city he escorted them. In different environs, in each conversation upon which they silently eavesdropped, the topic was the same: the death of a man for whom not one tear was shed. His passing was intermingled with banter about business, the weather, and even more trivial subjects.

"Jacob," the spirit's voice said solemnly.

"Yes, Spirit."

"I warn you, his time is nearly done. I fear he shall not pass his engagement with us with success."

"He will die?" Jacob asked.

"Yes. See."

They were in another place. There was nothing before them but a body, laid upon a bed and clearly lifeless, covered by a sheet. The spirit, by his pointing, demanded that Scrooge remove the sheet.

"This is the man about which all these parties have spoken?" Jacob asked.

"It is."

"Is it he? Is it Ebenezer?"

"It is."

Scrooge had not moved.

"I understand you," Scrooge said in response to the unspoken order to lift the sheet, "and I would do it, if I could. But I have not the power, Spirit. I have not the power."

"See," the spirit lamented. "He refuses to look upon his own fate. He pushes it away, as though it might pass him up if he but ignores it."

"But, Spirit," Jacob petitioned, "surely it does not all come down to this? Scrooge has torn his heart in shreds as he has seen what he has done. He shows an interest in Tiny Tim and his difficulties. Just because he cannot face the sight of his own earthly form, lifeless, he will not be given another chance?"

"It is not just this moment. It is all the moments. Despite all we have seen, he cannot comprehend that he is the one of whom they speak. If he cannot face his pain, he cannot hope to change. Even now, he appeals for this man as another man, not himself."

"If there is any person in the town who feels emotion caused by this man's death," cried Scrooge in agony, "show that person to me, Spirit, I beseech you!"

Jacob looked sadly upon Scrooge. "I mourn your death, dear friend," he said quietly. "I may be your sole mourner, but there is no less feeling in my heart for the loss of you than there would be in a church full of people. I am sorry, Ebenezer. For it was I who hastened your downfall. It was I who did not show care to your spirit. I mourn your death and everything I have done to make it such a cold and heartless experience."

The hooded spirit and his two charges again ventured out upon the streets, and once again found themselves at the doorstep of Bob Cratchit's home. As they started to pass inside, Jacob found himself restrained by the spirit.

"No, Jacob, this is for Scrooge alone."

"But he cannot see me. What does it matter if I join you?"

The spirit turned its hood toward the home. "It is

not for Ebenezer's sake that I hold you back, but for the sake of this good family. They suffer great loss. There is a crutch, now unused, by the fire. Even if they do not know you are here, their grief is personal. It is not for you to see."

When they emerged, Scrooge was even more shaken, and clearly mourning. The threesome moved on until they came to a churchyard. The graves there fit the mood of the evening. Stones marking the passage of men and women whom no one remembered were askew in different directions. Grass and weeds entangled the markers, slowly enveloping them in a careless prison. No feet had trodden these rows. No hands had left flowers or mementos to a life missed. All was dead about this place, its inhabitants, their memorials, and its future.

"Spirit, why are we here?" Jacob asked anxiously. "Is this part of Scrooge's learning?"

"His learning is finished."

Jacob could feel sorrow from the spirit. "Spirit, why do you weep? Scrooge seems willing to try to be a different man."

The ghost pointed to a single grave. He trembled, saying, "Jacob, I have no pleasure in this."

"But his feelings of regret, his pains of loss, his

feelings for Tiny Tim. Do these not count to his benefit in your eyes?"

"Scrooge mourns only for himself. For his lost opportunities. He has had his chance."

Jacob turned as he heard Scrooge petition the spirit. "Before I draw nearer to that stone to which you point, answer me one question. Are these the shadows of the things that will be, or are they shadows of things that may be, only?"

Jacob looked to the spirit, waiting for his answer.

To Scrooge, the ghost only pointed.

"Spirit!" Jacob said anxiously, "Spirit, you cannot bring him this far only to let him die!"

"Scrooge could not pass beyond his sorrow for his actions. If he cannot see that he must do more than feel regret—that he must do good—he does not partake of the peace we have to give him."

Scrooge edged toward the gravestone. "Men's courses will foreshadow certain ends, to which, if persevered in, they must lead," said Scrooge. "But if the courses be departed from, the ends will change. Say it is thus with what you show me!"

"Spirit," cried Jacob. "Say it is thus!"

"It is, but this change will not wait forever. Men's lives

are marked by time, and each is given enough. Even to-night, he might have extended his. But he did not see."

Scrooge had fallen to his knees as read his own name upon the gravestone. "Am I that man who lay upon the bed?" he cried.

The finger pointed from the grave to him, and back again.

Jacob nervously looked back and forth between the two.

"No, Spirit! Oh no, no!" cried Scrooge.

"No, Spirit," Jacob pleaded. "Listen to him. I believe he will yet change!"

Scrooge grasped at the spirit's robe and held fast, "Spirit, hear me, I am not the man I was. I will not be the man I must have been but for this intercourse. Why show me this, if I am past all hope!"

Jacob's demeanor suddenly calmed. He stood up straight and surveyed Scrooge upon the ground pleading for his future that was not to be. *Poor, dear friend*, Marley thought.

Then, with a sureness he had not known his entire life, he turned to the spirit. "If you need to settle a balance, if Scrooge is found wanting in his accounts with you, then balance your scale with me. I know he must learn, you have taught me so this night, but I believe he will change if you give him time. If you must, if you demand this justice, give me his chains. I will wear them with my own. I will carry them to all the places we both would have visited in our penance."

"Jacob . . ."

"Good Spirit," Scrooge cried out, as down upon the ground he fell before it, "Your nature intercedes for me, and pities me."

Jacob listened to Scrooge and looked down upon him with compassion. Firmly, he readdressed the spirit. "No, take me—give this man even if it is but one more day to honor the commitments he makes to you."

"You will wander forever, Jacob. You will not be back or visit us again. You have tasted of the bitterness of that world. And you go to it for him, forever, as he would have?"

"I do, Spirit."

"Assure me that I yet may change these shadows you have shown me, by an altered life!" Scrooge begged, unaware of the negotiation transpiring for his fate.

"I beseech thee, Spirit, give me his punishment, and give him my chance," Jacob implored.

Jacob held out his arms, prepared to take the weight

of Scrooge's links upon his own. The open hood turned toward Jacob. With Scrooge's sobs in the background, the trembling hand of the spirit reached out and grasped Jacob's hand. He squeezed it, and Jacob felt the love of this apparition fill him.

But, as Scrooge gave one final pleading, the spirit reluctantly released his grasp from Jacob as Scrooge took his other hand. When the spirit's fingers let go of Jacob, a transition began. The links of Scrooge's chain began to fall upon Jacob.

Scrooge sobbed, "I will honour Christmas in my heart, and try to keep it all the year."

Jacob's arms felt the increasing weight tearing at his spiritual limbs, but he did not cry out. He held his gaze fast upon Scrooge.

"I will live in the Past, the Present, and the Future," Scrooge committed to the spirit.

Around Jacob's shoulders the chains wound, adhering themselves to Jacob's chains and to himself. All the malice, all the hate, all the deceit of the years of Scrooge and Marley piled upon Jacob. With the weight of each link, Jacob felt he could bear no more. Suddenly, an image of a man he knew but had never seen came to his mind.

"Thelonius," Jacob said softly. "Help me bear this."

Unseen, but felt nonetheless, spirit hands reached out from a century before, not able to release the weights Jacob had taken upon himself, but holding him, steadying him against their pressure.

The mists began to return as he listened to Scrooge.

"The Spirits of all Three shall strive within me. I will not shut out the lessons that they teach."

Jacob began to fall back into the darkness that had held him for the last seven years. The mourning wails of the spirits in that place welled up in his ears.

Scrooge's voice started fading. "Oh, tell me I may sponge away the writing on this stone!"

Jacob uttered, "Be strong, my friend," as his image blended into the fog.

The spirit mourned the sorrow of the righteous and trembled with a vibration that shook Ebenezer, shook the gravestones in their loose places, shook the walls of the church that stood silent sentinel to this churchyard, and shook the bell in its steeple, causing it to peal boldly and painfully into the dark night, bearing solemn witness of what had happened here.

Scrooge held up his hands in pleading, unaware that his soul had already been saved.

II

Scrooge was repeating his pledge over and over before he realized he was in his bedchamber. The night was over, and sunlight streamed between the cracks of his shutters and around and under the folds of his curtain. Realizing where he was, he leapt from his bed and fell to the floor.

"Oh Jacob Marley! Heaven, and the Christmas Time be praised for this! I say it on my knees, old Jacob; on my knees!"

He danced about the room, reveling in this new morning of his life. He was sharp in his recognition of everything about him. He was giddy and excited, and he laughed a laugh that had been imprisoned in him for many years.

Not knowing what day it was, he ran to the window and threw open the shutters, the sparkling sunlight bathing his face and the tears still present from his last encounter with the spirit.

"What's today?" he called to a young boy below.

"Eh?"

"What's today, my fine fellow?" repeated Scrooge with enthusiasm.

"Today! Why, Christmas Day!"

Old dear Scrooge began at that very moment to honor Christmas the way he had promised. With every breath he would take from that moment forward, Ebenezer would wrap his heart around the sacred holiday and around all he could find who stood in need of his care. That day, he made peace with the passersby on his street who had known him only for the cold miser he had been. He made peace with the needy as he provided enough donations not only to feed a countless number but to knock the breath out of the faithful men who had sought him out to provide alms for relief. He made peace with his nephew, Fred, who had suffered all these years for the good of his uncle's soul, and he attended what would be the first of many Christmas dinners with his family. He made peace with the Cratchits, surprising them with the grandest Christmas feast there ever was and raising Bob's wages, assuring him a job that would no longer rob his family of the comfort of security. As for Tiny Tim—well, as has been told us, Tim did not die and gained himself a second father. Scrooge was as good as his word, and while some laughed at him, and others would not release him from their judgments of his former self, he paid them no mind and went about doing all the good he could find.

But what of Jacob?

Jacob opened his eyes in the mist. He could not help but smile. He knew what to expect now, and though the weight of his new punishment would be severe, he would be able to bear it, knowing that Scrooge was free.

The weight. As he thought of it, he realized there was no greater weight. Just a moment ago he had felt the chains forged in Scrooge's life heaped upon his frame. But now they were gone, and, upon further inspection, he realized that his chains were gone too. He did not know if he was sitting or lying down, but he stood and felt a freedom unknown to him since his boyhood. He looked about, and the mists lightened.

Slowly, a form came into his view. It was the hooded

spectre. As he watched, the black and dreary robes began to lighten. They went to gray, to ash, to white, and then beyond white, the only description of which would be facilitated by words that do not exist. Their brilliance banished all the mists about them. Two hands emerged from the arms of the robe and reached up. Slowly they pulled back the hood, and, to Jacob's complete surprise, there stood the beautiful, kindly man who had greeted him on the day of his death.

For a long time, they just stood and looked upon each other. Jacob could see that the spirit before him was crying.

"Why do you cry, and why am I here? I don't understand. Where are Scrooge's chains? And where are mine? Scrooge is free, is he not?"

The spirit smiled. "Scrooge is free. At least, he has been freed from his past and now may redeem himself by his own actions." The spirit laughed. "And, if the first day of his freedom is any indication, he is well on his way."

The spirit paused as he looked at Jacob with admiration. "Do you understand what you did?"

Jacob understood, but said nothing.

"Jacob, you gave all for your fellow man. Greater love does not exist. You laid down your life for a friend. Your sacrifice satisfied the demands of justice. Jacob, you too are now free."

Jacob fell into the spirit's arms, and the two cried tears of joy for goodness and its effect on men.

I3

More than twenty-five years passed. Scrooge kept working in the countinghouse, but it might have been a new profession.

Oddly, he did fulfill the warning Marley had given him so many years ago. He became known as an easy mark. When his debtors fell into trouble, Scrooge was the first to help them through. Many supposed that Scrooge's kindness was taken advantage of at times, but he paid it no matter. For all he lost in that kindness, he seemed to gain in the process. Some of his old acquaintances at the Exchange, while admiring his increased business, would offer under their breaths that perhaps he would be a good deal more profitable if he were tougher on some of his clients. He heard them, and he didn't care.

The journey from his old home to the countinghouse now took Ebenezer three times longer to make than before that night of nights. The distance had not lengthened, nor had a new route been chosen. Rather, this grand old man would stop to pay a word of kindness to each passerby. It had begun with the poulterer, with whom he had built a special bond that merry Christmas morning he had purchased the prize turkey for the feast at the Cratchit home. Each day, as he passed, he waved to Big John and asked him how he was. More remarkably, he waited for an answer. He knew of John's aches and pains, his loves and losses. He laughed with him as he bounced John's children and, in later years, his grandchildren, on his knee, and cried with him at the funeral of John's wife. To John, Scrooge was truly a friend to whom he could turn in all circumstances, and to Scrooge, John was that friend as well.

From there he made the acquaintance of others, bidding each a good day and querying after their health. For each new face, he would make introductions and ask them something about themselves, and from that day forward, upon seeing them in the road or the market, he could call them by name and warm their hands and hearts.

It so raised the spirits of that little corner of London that the shopkeepers and their customers would come to their doors as Scrooge passed by to wave and to receive the morning greetings from the good old man of Christmas.

And Christmas! Oh, what a fuss Scrooge would make! The countinghouse would be festooned with holly and boughs of fir and poinsettia. Scrooge would not leave home or warehouse without his pockets stuffed with candy canes for the young lads and lasses who found their way into his path.

He was oft heard to ask of a good man or woman, while gesturing toward a young person dressed in rags, what they knew of the person's situation. Would they have food for Christmas? He would visit with pastors and priests and rabbis and quietly find the names and addresses of those who might be hungry at that special time.

Then, each year, around the twenty-second of December, he would walk into Big John's shop and recite the same script. "You know, John, it just isn't right that anyone should feel the pains of hunger on Christmas Day." Handing him a carefully prepared list, crafted with the precision of a man who had managed well his accounts for years, he would say, "If you would deliver a goose to each of these families, I would appreciate it." Then, with a twinkle, he would hand John an envelope containing payment for the birds and extra for John's family and whisper, "I wish to remain anonymous," never failing to laugh at the irony of his own joke.

On the twenty-fourth of December, Big John would amass his army of young men—not a one paid, but assembled for the love of the old man, and many the recipients of his anonymous gift in years past—and they would fan out from the shop in untold directions to untold numbers of little streets, to knock upon untold numbers of doors and yell, "Hallo in there, I've a Christmas gift for you."

The objects of Scrooge's generosity would answer the door, and, upon seeing the carefully wrapped goose, they would scream and cry and laugh and pray at the sight of their sustenance. And, when told the giver wished to remain anonymous, they would bid blessings upon old Ebenezer, the founder of the feast and the most well-known anonymous man in London.

Finally, the young men would return to Big John's, cram a carriage from floor to ceiling with the headless fowl, and travel with John to the poorhouses and work-houses and leave in their kitchens gifts of food. The doors of the carriage, lent each year to the occasion, were covered with butcher paper, but behind it, everyone knew it was painted with the words "Marley & Scrooge."

Only after Scrooge saw, peeking from the darkened windows of the countinghouse, the carriage and parade of poultry pull away would he step out into the Christmas night and begin his walk to Fred's for their annual Christmas dinner.

Time passed, and the young boys who had plied his pockets for candy canes were now fathers themselves, and had at least once brought their young children to bid good day to Uncle Ebenezer.

It seems to be true among all who are given the blessing of a gradual death that there is, in their final months or weeks, an instinct that drives them to tie up loose ends relative to worldly possessions. For the greedy, it is to hoard, for what purpose nobody knows, and for good reason they cannot tell for there is none. But for the generous, such as good old Scrooge had become, it is a chance to leave in the world those things of the world, to do good in the world after they are gone. It was in the spring of his eighty-third year that Scrooge felt that prompting to tie up his earthly matters.

By then, Ebenezer was becoming frail, the walk from his home to the countinghouse becoming slower and more painful, despite the joys afforded to him in the journey. Fred, ever watchful of his uncle, noticed the increasing difficulty of his step and invited Scrooge to come live with them and give up his time at the countinghouse. Fred was a bit surprised to find no protest in the old, gentle man. Fred and Bob Cratchit now ran the firm as his partners and were doing a very satisfactory job of it. Scrooge mainly offered guidance in between his caring conversations with their clients.

It was in this situation, on the occasion of a beautiful spring day, that Scrooge decided to pack up his office. For all his past years of miserliness, he had accumulated very little in the way of goods, and for the more recent past years of generosity, he had given most of it away. This purging, then, required only the better part of a morning.

While Fred and Bob labored in the front office, he worked slowly, contemplating each item he picked up, trying to see what good it could be put to in the service of someone else. Having completed sorting through all but one of his desk drawers, he leaned down to pull out the final one. Upon doing so, he paused as he stared at his old cash box within it.

He had not opened that box since his night with the spirits, and yet he knew its contents as though he had closed it moments ago. Beneath its cover there was an inset removable shelf. On it, to the left, would sit some rare coins of the realm. He would give these to Fred's youngest son, Jonathan, who at fourteen collected everything from frogs to wax stamps. To the right, most likely some amount of cash, saved for an emergency that never came. This he would give to Fred's wife to offset the cost of his pending stay with them.

That shelf would lift out of the box, and beneath it lay a velvet-lined compartment. It was the contents of this part of the box that had slowed his breathing and held him in abeyance from opening the lid. In that soft cradle lay a ring, the promise of which had long ago been broken, past and buried. He had intended to sell the ring when gold prices improved, yet upon each rise in value, he found he could not. It held him somehow, painfully, to life as it should have been. He could see every facet of it, though he had not yet opened the lid.

To whom could he give this ring? Surely, its value had increased over time. Gold was worth many times over what it had been when Belle had placed the ring with its precious stone in his shaking hand. But it carried too much sadness to bequeath to anyone, and he feared the history of the ring, known or not, might somehow pass on its sorrow in some unknown way.

He held his breath and opened the box, finding everything as he had seen it in his memory. He slowly lifted the shelf, and his eyes moistened with tears as the glint of the ring reached him. He lifted it and rolled it between his fingers, remembering the moment almost sixty years ago in which his resolve to marry Belle had withered before Marley's insinuations of Ebenezer's own failings in judgment for wanting marriage. The ring, as a ring, was dead.

Suddenly, a thought struck his mind. To do good, it must be changed, refined to its core elements and made to offer some service in a new form, leaving behind what it had stood for but had been lost.

Placing the ring in his pocket, he rose, retrieved his cane, and went into the office. "Fred," he asked, "would you have the time to go somewhere with me this morning?"

Fred looked up. "What? Of course, Uncle. Where shall we go?"

"I will show you. Just come along if you could."

Together they stepped into the beautiful morning for the long, slow walk on Ebenezer's errand.

They first went to the assayer's office. As they entered, the clerk was busy at his desk, face buried in his calculations, when he heard the sharp "plunk" of something dropped into the scale in front of him. Looking up with a start, he saw Ebenezer staring at him intently.

For many years, this man had hated the moment Scrooge walked into his office, knowing he would be bargained down to unreasonable levels of exchange. Then, one day, he had been shocked as Scrooge had showed up not with metal to trade but with an envelope. Scrooge had handed him the package and simply said, "I owe you an apology, Perrins. This should make up for all the value you lost in your transactions with me, with a bit of interest." Then sternly he had added, "You know I keep meticulous records. Do not question me on the value in that envelope. I will take no haggling." With that, Scrooge had walked out. Perrins had opened the envelope, expecting to find such a pittance as to create insult as its primary purpose. However, he had nearly fainted as he found enough money to cover the differences, as Scrooge had said, and interest, as Scrooge had wanted to name it, that was worth many times over the original gap between actuality and fairness.

This day, Scrooge wore a friendly smile as he sat in the chair opposite Perrins and said, "Mr. Perrins, this is an old piece of jewelry that has never served its purpose, and is now ready to do something useful. I assure you the value will not go to me, but to somewhere needed. What can you give me for it?"

Mr. Perrins looked at the scale, back at Scrooge, and then casually put a few counterweights on the scale until it balanced. He summed the values in his mind, opened a folder and read a few figures, made a few notes on a receipt, and handed it to Scrooge, who looked down at the numbers.

"Mr. Perrins, I ask for nothing more than what is fair. This is far too much."

Mr. Perrins looked into Scrooge's eyes and simply said, "Percy."

"What?" Scrooge asked in confusion.

"Percy," he said again. "My name is Percy, and I wish you would call me that rather than Mr. Perrins. Then I can feel that this is just what it is supposed to be, a gift between friends."

Scrooge struggled to stand up as Mr. Perrins came

around the desk and helped him by the elbow. Scrooge took his hand in a warm embrace. "Ebenezer, Percy. Call me Ebenezer."

Scrooge took his receipt and went to the cashier's office to claim its worth in pounds. After bidding his hellos and good-byes, he and Fred set out for his next destination.

Even in a city such as London, scarred by coal soot and the occasional building left untended, spring would not be deterred from its renewing warmth. As Ebenezer walked, the peace of the morning filled him with joy, which was why he was so startled with the contrast when they arrived at the graveyard.

Here was a bit of winter, dogged in its resolve to hold its ground cold against the spring. Where the fresh air seemed to waft this way and that down every street, it turned in its journey at this spot, curling around but not through the gray place of death and sorrow.

Scrooge walked slowly between tilted and broken headstones, pushing away dead branches with his cane as he stepped. Fred followed at his side. Finally they came to an open spot, where Scrooge stopped and looked at the ground quietly. "This is the place I wish to be buried," Scrooge said.

"Here? This graveyard is for the poor. Why, you know we have a beautiful spot for you at All Saints Church. You don't need to be here."

Scrooge said nothing of the experiences he had had on this spot, pleading with the hooded spectre for his soul. He simply said to Fred, "This spot is sacred to me, for reasons I cannot share, and for other reasons I feel profoundly but do not understand. This is where I would like to be buried."

"So it will be, Uncle."

"Fred, I would like to see another grave while we are here. Walk this way," he said, pointing with his cane.

They shuffled slowly down two more aisles. When they stopped, Scrooge's eyes filled with tears. Before them, a thin stone, the type provided for those without a penny to pay for a proper burial, had been broken in two. On the first half, the letters etched into it read *Mar,* and on the second, *ley.* No first name, no epitaph. Only the single last name, broken.

"Jacob," Scrooge said softly to the lonely grave, "I am sorry. I have not been here since the day we buried you." Scrooge corrected himself with a smile and said, "Well, except briefly for one evening, but you may have been told about that." Fred stood by, listening without understanding. "I would like to do something for you."

Scrooge stood and surveyed the graveyard. "Blessed are the poor . . ." he said softly.

Scrooge went to the parish vicar and made arrangements for a new headstone for Jacob, acquired a plot for himself (though wouldn't the priest be unnerved to know Scrooge had already been buried there once!), and left funds to repair or replace all the stones in the yard, improve the walks and the grounds, and plant flowers in the spring.

Later that day, he made his way to his new home in Fred's house.

The months passed and Scrooge grew weaker, and as he did, his peace increased. Upon contemplation, he never could release the feelings of sorrow for what he had lost, but that pain was always followed by gratefulness for his second chance and these almost three decades of joy.

The Christmas season approached one final time for Ebenezer. Early in December, on an unseasonably pleasant day, he called for Fred.

"My good nephew, the priest of the old church we visited sent me a note. The work has all been done, and he is quite proud of the result and thinks it would do me well to see how it has changed. I would like to go there tomorrow. Would you allow Fan to join me?"

"Uncle, are you quite sure? That walk is far for you, and Fan, while keeping you great company in her conversation, will not be much help if you fall."

"I will be much help!" they both heard from the doorway to Scrooge's room.

Fred smiled as his beautiful, strong-willed, twelve-year-old daughter, Fan, stood with defiance. After a gaggle of boys, Fred and his wife had been blessed with one last child, a girl. Though neither said a word, Fred and Scrooge smiled at each other, knowing that her resolve aptly earned Fan her name.

The next day, with Fan watching every step, Scrooge made his way back to the graveyard, where the priest met them and escorted them through the rows of stones standing at uniform attention, the grounds bearing silent and polite homage to the lives within their grasp. Scrooge walked from row to row until he came to Marley's headstone, a substantial affair. With satisfaction he read, "Jacob Thelonius Marley," his birth and death dates, and the simple inscription: "My Friend."

The priest took Scrooge's elbow and said, "Come,

Mr. Scrooge, there is someone I think you would like to meet."

They walked a few rows over to find a woman standing before one of the newly replaced stones, fresh poinsettia laid at its base.

"Mrs. Higbee, I want you to meet someone. This is Ebenezer Scrooge. He paid for all these renovations, including the refurbishing of your husband's grave."

The elderly woman turned slowly to look at Scrooge. Her face showed the effects of many hard years, but her blue eyes were bright. Slowly, she summoned the words that would express her gratefulness. "Sir, this is wonderful. I loved my husband very much, but we were not people of any means, and I was never able to pay for a respectful place to lay him. How do I thank you for this?"

Scrooge took her by the hand and smiled warmly. "You are most welcome, Mrs. Higbee. It is indeed a great thank you to me to see your happiness with it all. You have made my day brighter."

Then he paused. "Higbee. I know that name somehow, but . . ." laughing at himself, " . . . there is a great deal I knew that I don't seem to know anymore."

"Ain't it just the way it is?" she smiled. "I think it's a gift to us older ones, really. It allows us to treasure what is worth remembering and easily let go of all that doesn't really matter anymore."

She looked back at her husband's grave, and then looked at Scrooge again. Without a word, she reached under her muffler at the back of her neck and unfastened something. She then held out a necklace with a single pearl suspended from it.

"Sir, this was a gift to me from my husband. It would please me greatly if you would take it with my thanks."

Scrooge's old eyes opened wider than they had perhaps since he had first seen Jacob pass through his door. "That necklace! It belonged to my sister! I gave it to her myself. Where did you come across it?"

She smiled as she looked at the necklace now in Scrooge's hands. "My Richard was a wonderful man, but oh, he could not keep a shilling firmly in his grasp. He had given me a beautiful engagement ring when he was a young businessman, but even before we were married, it was repossessed and he was thrown in debtor's prison. I had promised myself to Richard, and a promise is a promise, so I waited, several years, until he had paid his debts and we could be married. Never again did we have enough money for things, but no matter, we were so in love! Richard became a carpenter, and he was quite good at it. Some years ago, our church had been given an old desk for the priest to use in his offices. One drawer did not close well, and the priest, knowing my Richard's skills, asked him to see if he could repair it. Richard found that the drawer did not close because there was a hidden compartment that somehow had come askew. When he opened it to make the repairs, he found this inside, wrapped in an old piece of paper. He showed the priest, who knew our meager situation and told him to take it as thanks for being willing to do the work for nothing."

She sighed and smiled. "And, that evening, he gave it to me. It was the only other nice thing he was able to give me. But you know, Mr. Scrooge, it didn't matter at all. It was the love behind it that gave its value to me."

"But, your church, where did the desk come from, and how did the necklace get in it?" Scrooge asked, still amazed.

"I don't know that, I am sorry," she said. "But Mr. Scrooge, things have a way of coming to rights, don't they, now? This little necklace seems determined to do some good. A gift from you to your sister. Probably a gift from her to someone for some kindness shared. And so forth and so forth until today, when I want to give it to you."

Scrooge protested. "Please, you keep it. My sister has passed, and it has great meaning for you." Then, thinking a minute, he said, "Mrs. Higbee, I know the value of that necklace—you could have sold it and done all I did here, and more."

Mrs. Higbee looked lovingly at the necklace still resting in his open palm. "Oh, but Mr. Scrooge. I could not sell this. The value of this pearl would be lost in trading it for money. It is only in the giving of it that its true worth can be shared." She persisted. "You take it. It isn't often we get second chances. You have been given a rare opportunity to offer it twice. Give it to another young woman whose heart will be lifted by its beauty, and by your kindness." She smiled at Fan as she spoke.

Scrooge took the necklace and thanked Mrs. Higbee, walking back to the small patch of ground that would be his grave. He turned to Fan, who had silently followed him.

"Fan, I think Mrs. Higbee had an excellent idea, don't you? I would like you to have this. As I said, I gave it to my sister, your grandmother—oh my goodness, think about it." He did some calculations in his head. "Fan, I gave it to her sixty-six years ago, when she, like you, was twelve. I spent all the money I had on it. It was a gift to her to thank her for never giving up on me."

"Uncle Ebenezer, this is beautiful! You called her Little Fan, didn't you, Uncle? I have her name!"

"That is right, Fan, I called her Little Fan. And you deserve her name. You are sweet and pure," and then, smiling, "and strong, just like her."

"I love it, Uncle!"

"I love you, Fan. And whenever you wear it, you remember what it stands for."

She reached up on her tiptoes, put her arms around his neck, and kissed his cheek. "I love you, dear, dear Uncle."

Fan and Ebenezer slowly made their way back to Fred's home, pausing dozens of times for Scrooge to pay his respects to those he knew and to meet those he did not. Fan patiently waited each time, holding his elbow, and starting to cry for how much she was going to miss her wonderful uncle.

• • •

It is said that nature loves order, and, if left to its devices, it will put things where and when it wants them to be. A few weeks later, as the sun set on Christmas Eve,

Ebenezer Scrooge, beloved man of the people, gave up the ghost.

His funeral was two days later. The old church was filled. All the men, women, and children in attendance were both mourning and cheerful—sad for the loss of their friend, but happy, too, for Uncle Ebenezer had often said that when he died, he wanted people to see just how blessed a man could be by his friends. So many in that congregation did not know each other, but they all knew Scrooge. In the front row sat his family: Fred, his wife, his sons, and his daughter, Fan, and beside them, good old Bob Cratchit, his wife, and their children and families. It must of course be noted that at the end of that row, a tall and strong man, the one to whom Scrooge had been a second father, sat with his wife and cradled his new son, Timothy Ebenezer Cratchit.

At the end of the memorial, each member of the congregation passed before the coffin, leaving tears and thanks for this man who had made such a difference in his or her life. Shopkeepers and bankers, poor and rich, old friends and newly acquainted—to each of these Scrooge had given something of himself, and they blessed him for it.

The crowd dispersed in time, and in the huge chapel

only one man stood by Scrooge. "Dear Uncle," Fred said with tears in his eyes, "you kept the day and taught us all."

With a smile, he said, "And did it all with Merry Christmas on your lips."

Fred gently patted Ebenezer's cold cheek and then reached into his own breast pocket, taking out a sprig of holly he had carried here for this occasion. He carefully placed it in Scrooge's hand, wrapping the lifeless fingers about its stem, and then gently moved the hand with its precious gift over the good old man's heart.

14

As we have spent so much time with the spirits in this little tale, perhaps we could venture just a bit further. If the funeral of Scrooge was a day of sorrow, his welcome beyond death was twice that over with joy.

That final Christmas Eve, Scrooge lay back upon his cot and smiled. *I have had a good life,* he thought to himself. He listened with pleasure to the sounds of family, his family, in the other rooms. Although they had spent every minute of the last few weeks with him, by some circumstance he now found himself alone. This pleased him, as he could tell his time had come and he wished to bid farewell to this wonderful world on his own.

He closed his eyes as he felt something comfortable

begin to envelop him. Then he heard bells. At first, he thought they were church bells, but there were all kinds and types, ringing with abandon.

"Hmm," he mused aloud, "it reminds me of the night Jacob visited me."

"It should!"

Ebenezer opened his eyes with a start. He was no longer in his bedroom in Fred's home, but surrounded by some vast landscape he could not make out, knowing only that it was pleasant. Standing before him was Jacob Thelonius Marley. He was straight and tall, his hair the color of a raven. No bandage wrapped his head. No chains weighed him down.

The two men looked silently at each other for a while, the understanding of years on either side of the veil passing between them.

Ebenezer spoke first. "Jacob! You look a good bit better than the last time I saw you!"

Jacob smiled at his old friend. "Not more gravy than grave about me?"

"No, and not a bit of moldy cheese!"

The men approached each other. As they came close, Jacob put his hand upon Ebenezer's shoulder.

"Ebenezer, I am sorry—"

"No, no, Jacob," Scrooge interrupted him. "Say no more. You have nothing to be sorry for. You saved my life. Not a day has gone by that I have not praised your name for your visit in my behalf. Whatever you did, whatever we did, that led to the necessity of that evening has passed and is settled. All I know is that because of you, I began to live."

Scrooge paused for a moment, then added, "Jacob Marley, you are a good, good man."

Jacob nodded, and both men smiled.

After a few moments, Jacob put his hand out to show the way to somewhere. "Come, Ebenezer, there is a great deal to do! We have our work cut out for us, old friend."

There was in fact a great deal more good to do, as Marley said, and they did it with all their hearts. It was said among the spirits that if there was a lost soul that needed reaching, if there was a hard, cold man or woman who was most likely beyond redemption, if anyone could help them, Jacob Thelonius Marley and Ebenezer Scrooge could do it. Sometimes the spirits that assisted them called Marley *Scrooge*, and sometimes Scrooge *Marley*. But they each answered to both names—it was all the same to them.

And to this day, when we find ourselves in the right

place at the right time to assist a poor wayfarer on the path of life, a moment's pause may recall the story of good old Scrooge and good old Marley, and our hearts may be softened, we may stop to listen, and we may even offer a hand of kindness to the one who just happens, by some circumstance, to cross our path.